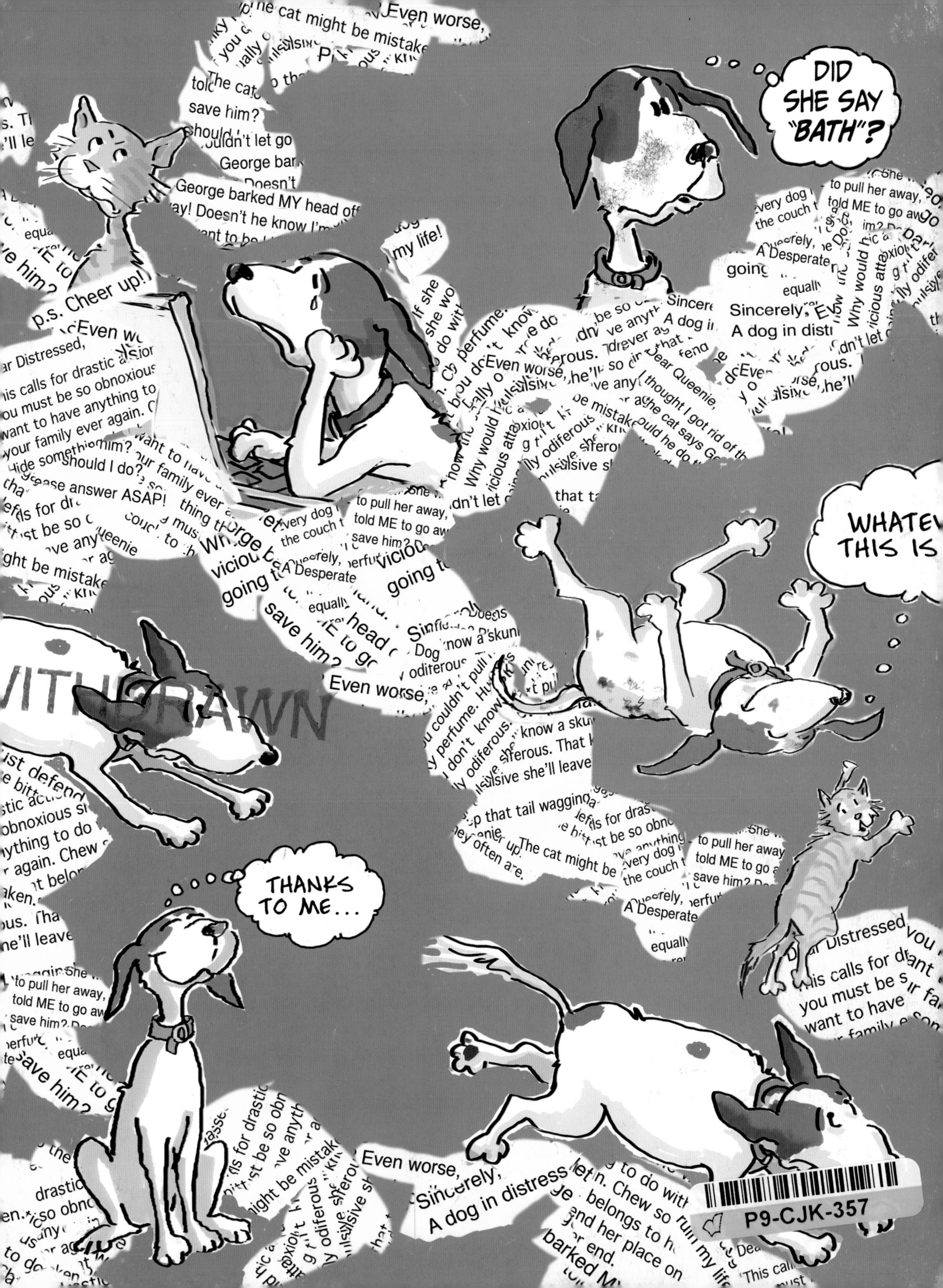
DID SHE SAY "BATH"?
WHATE THIS IS
THANKS TO ME...

Clarion Books
215 Park Avenue South
New York, New York 10003
Copyright © 2010 by Eileen Christelow

The illustrations were executed in digital media.
The text was set in Fold and Staple.

For information about permission to
reproduce selections from this book, write
to Permissions, Houghton Mifflin Harcourt
Publishing Company, 215 Park Avenue South,
New York, New York 10003.

Clarion Books is an imprint of Houghton
Mifflin Harcourt Publishing Company.

www.hmhbooks.com

Library of Congress Cataloging-in-Publication Data

Christelow, Eileen.
The desperate dog writes again / Eileen
Christelow.
p. cm.
Summary: When a new girlfriend comes
between Emma the dog and her owner George,
Emma e-mails "Ask Queenie," an advice column
for dogs having problems with difficult humans.
ISBN 978-0-547-24205-7
[1. Dogs—Fiction. 2. Advice columns—Fiction.]
I. Title.

PZ7.C4523De 2010
[E]—dc22

2009035113

Manufactured in China

LEO 10 9 8 7 6 5 4 3 2 1

4500226594

THE DESPERATE DOG WRITES AGAIN

EILEEN CHRISTELOW

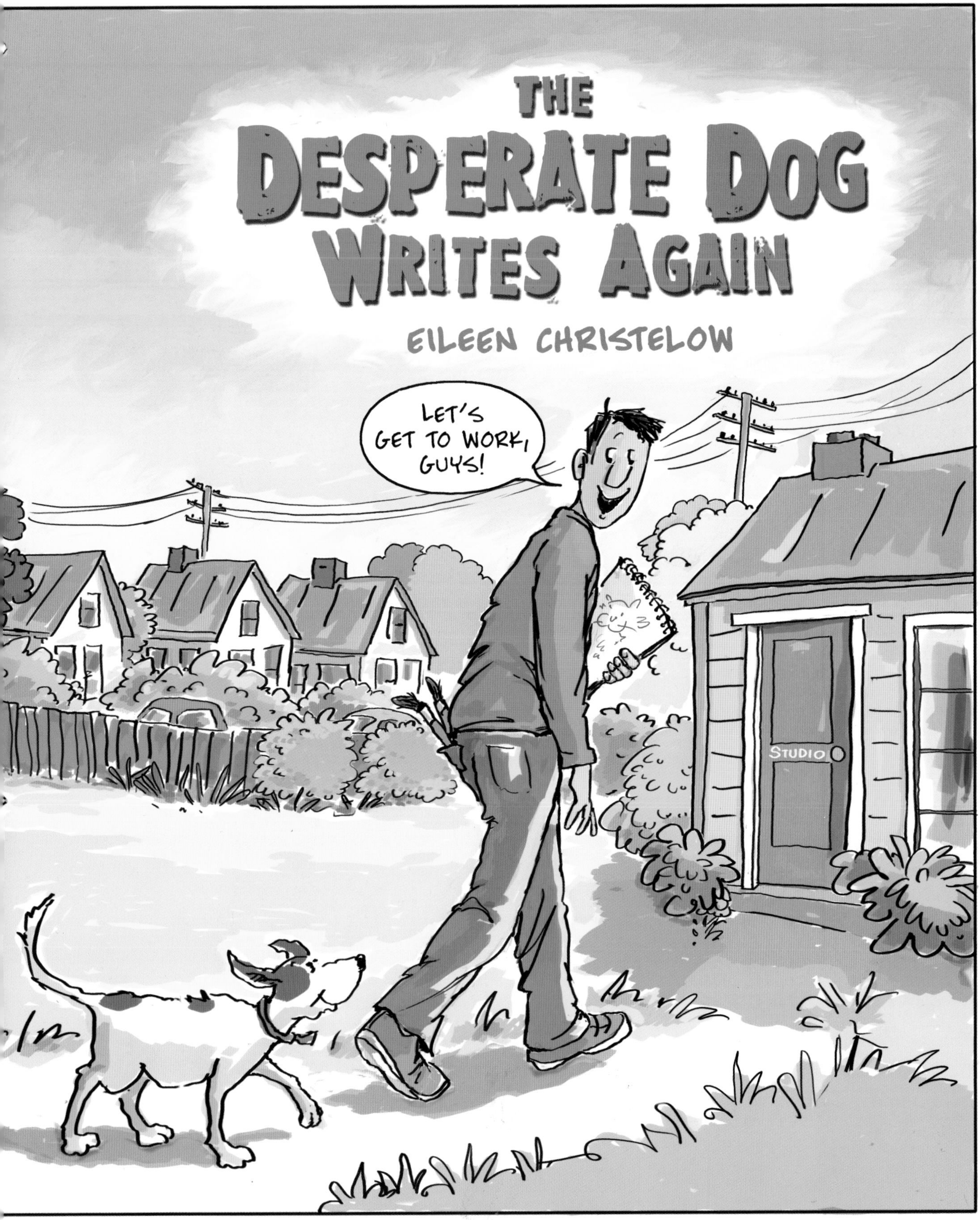
LET'S GET TO WORK, GUYS!
STUDIO

CLARION BOOKS
HOUGHTON MIFFLIN HARCOURT • BOSTON • NEW YORK • 2010

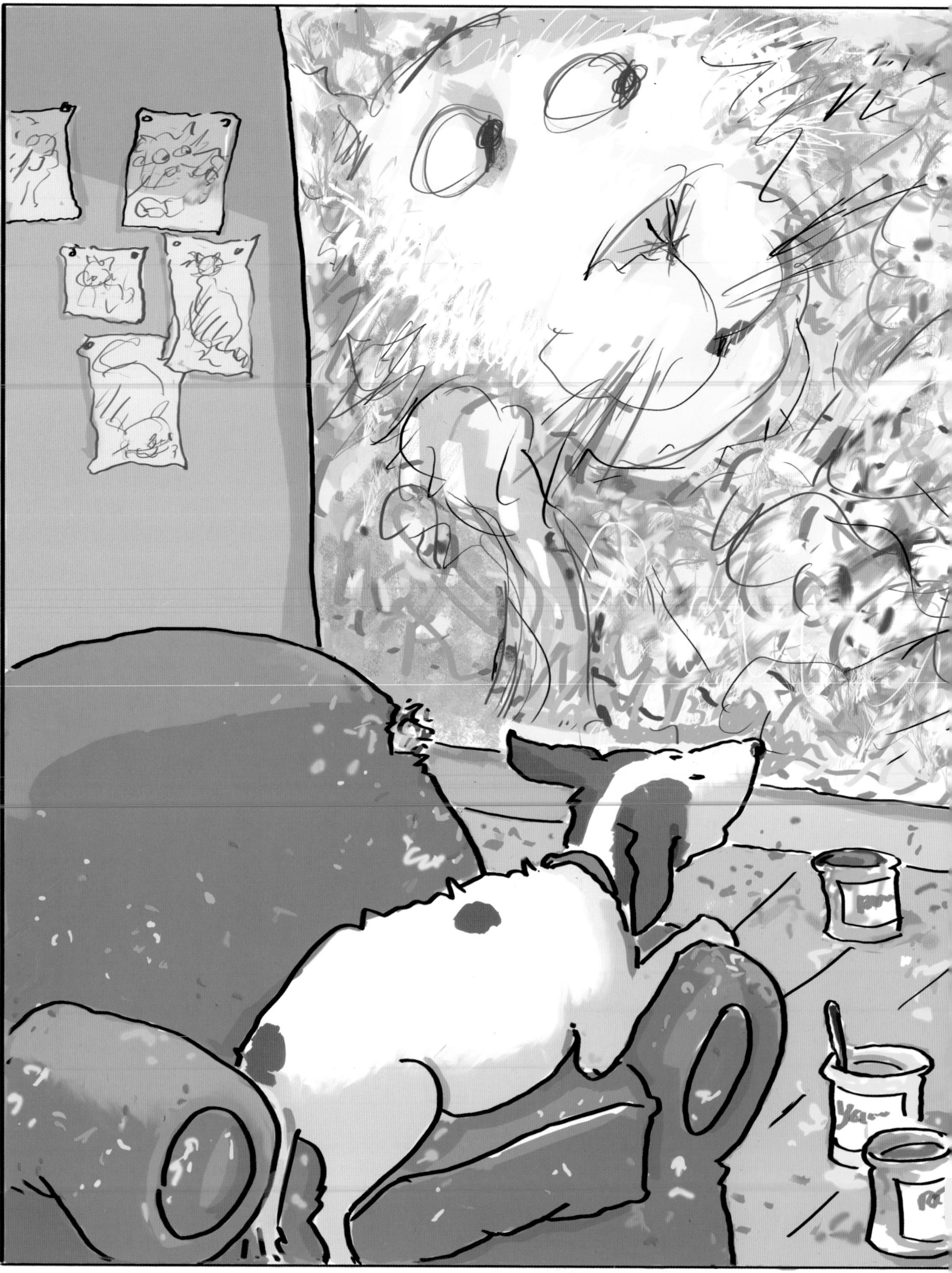

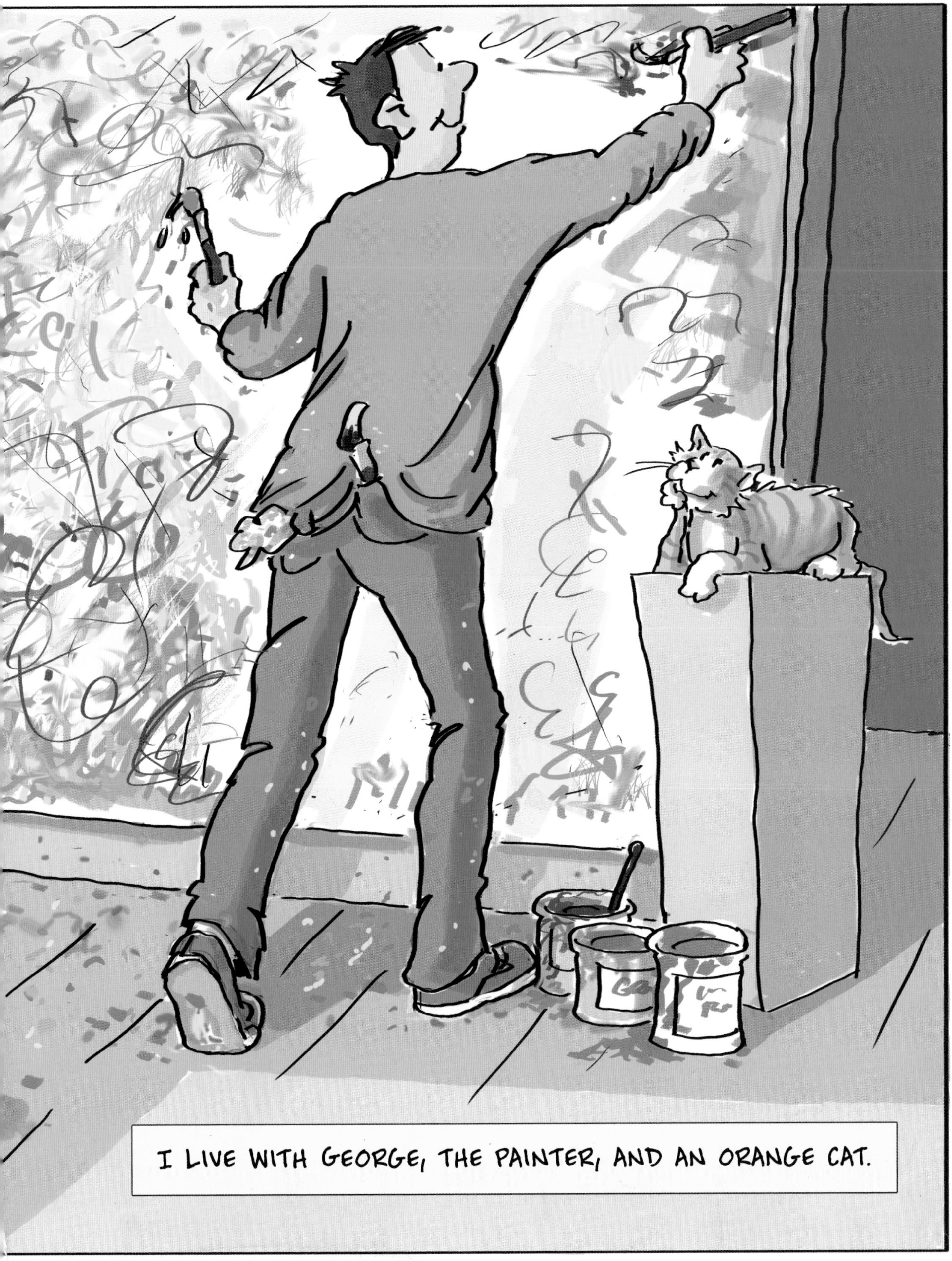
I LIVE WITH GEORGE, THE PAINTER, AND AN ORANGE CAT.

MOST TIMES, WE ARE A HAPPY FAMILY.

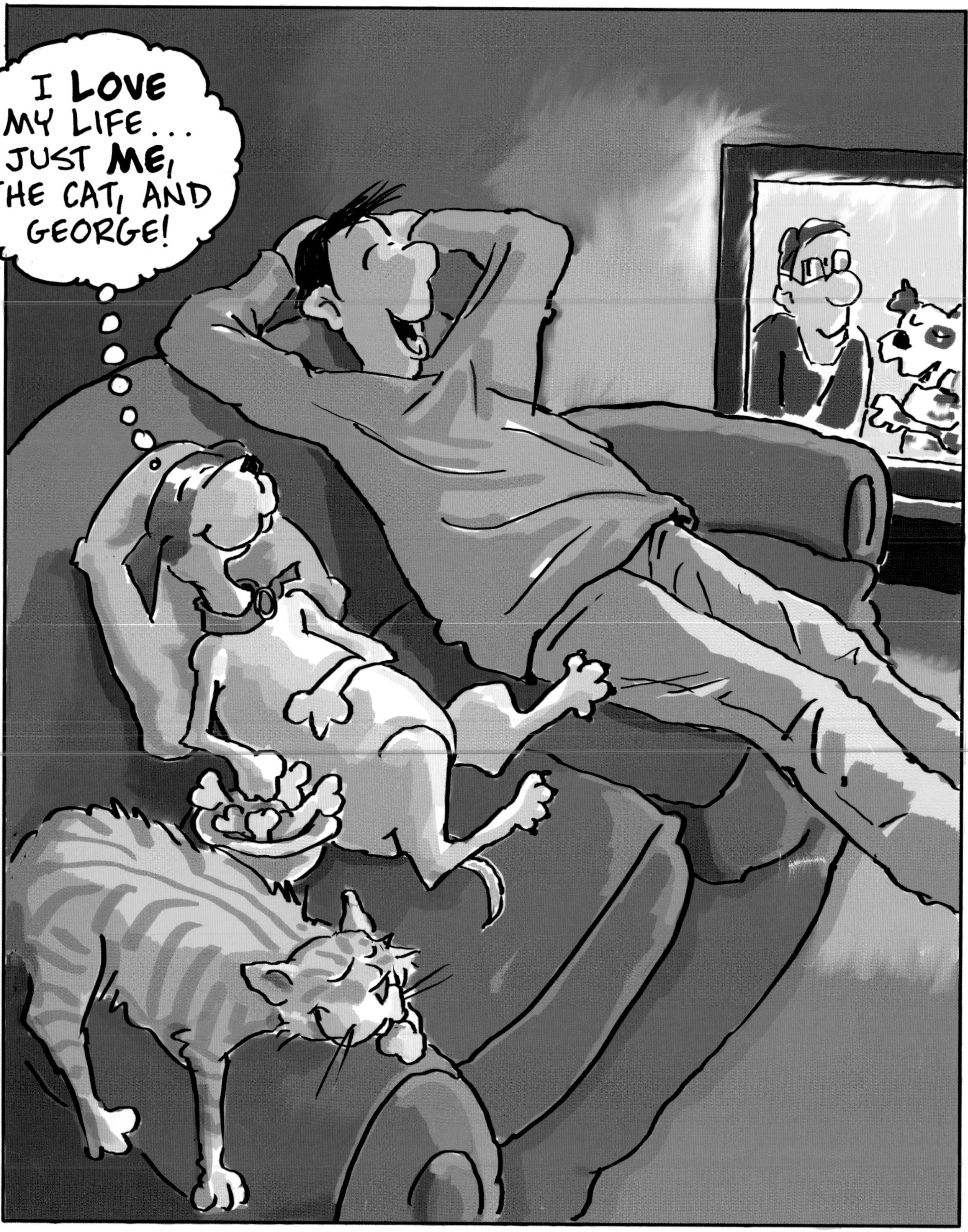
I **LOVE** MY LIFE... JUST **ME**, THE CAT, AND GEORGE!

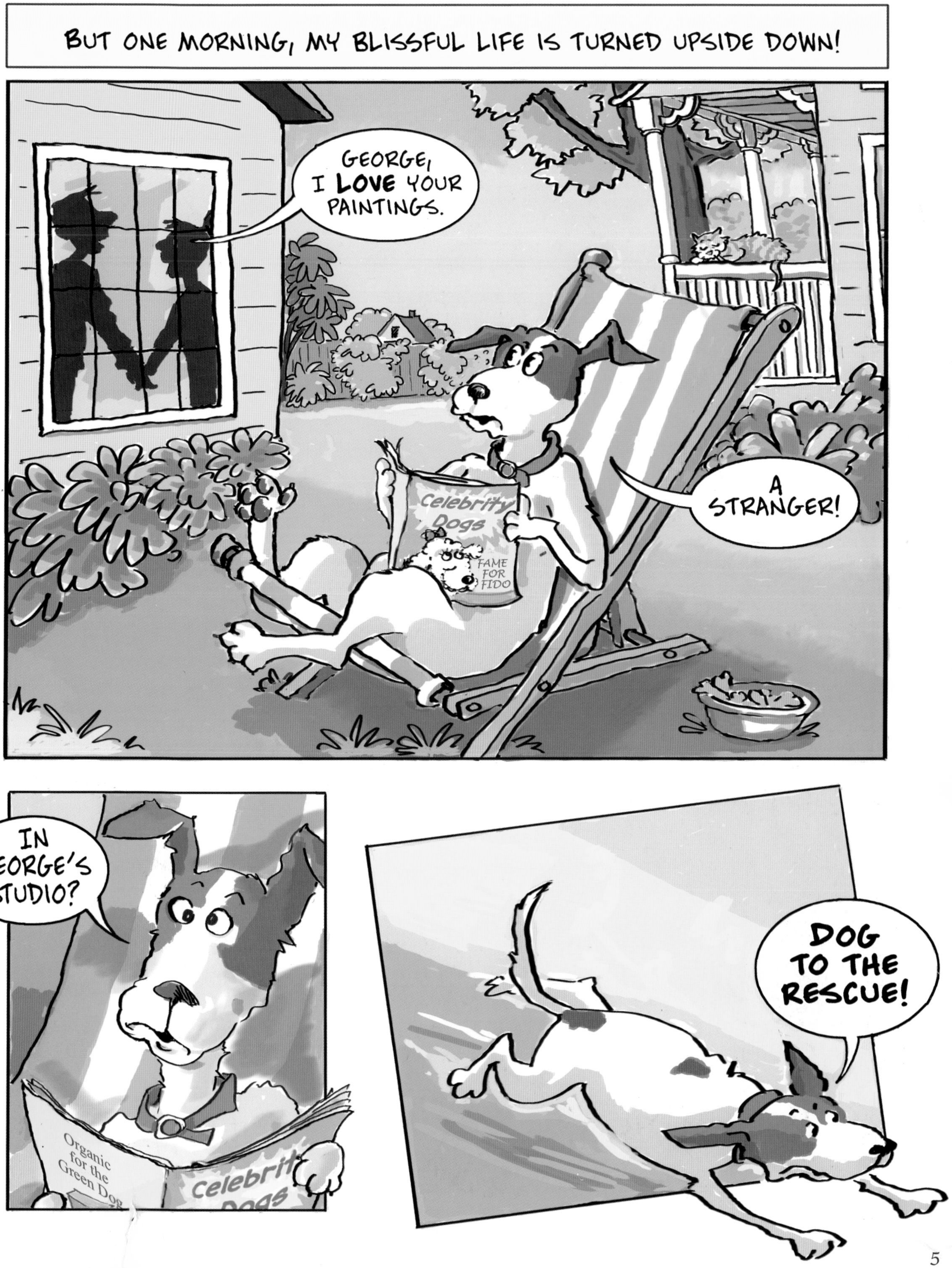
BUT ONE MORNING, MY BLISSFUL LIFE IS TURNED UPSIDE DOWN!
GEORGE, I **LOVE** YOUR PAINTINGS.
Celebrity Dogs
FAME FOR FIDO
A STRANGER!
IN GEORGE'S STUDIO?
Organic for the Green Dog
DOG TO THE RESCUE!

I DISCOVER A WOMAN . . . HOLDING GEORGE'S HAND!

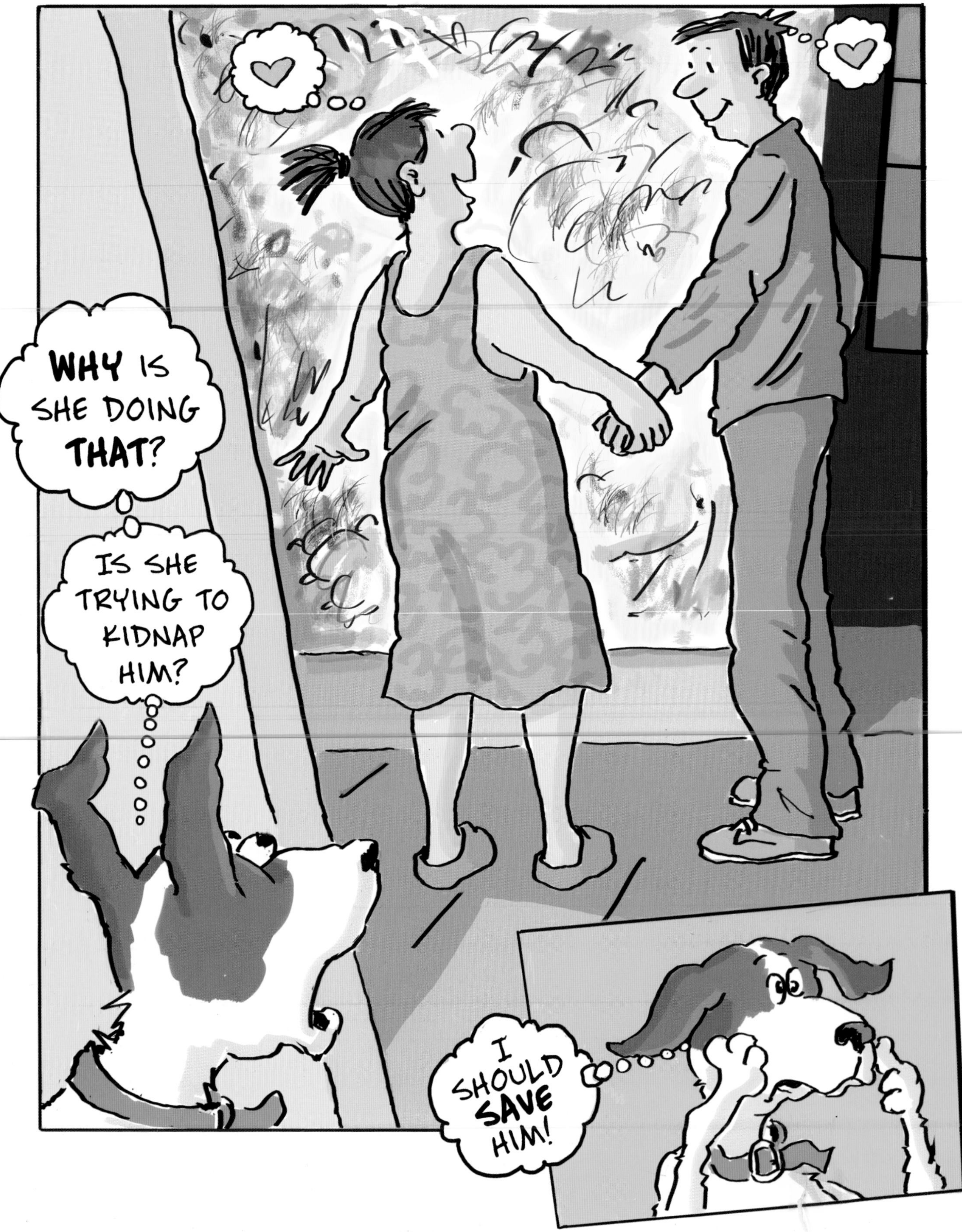
WHY IS SHE DOING THAT?
IS SHE TRYING TO KIDNAP HIM?
I SHOULD SAVE HIM!

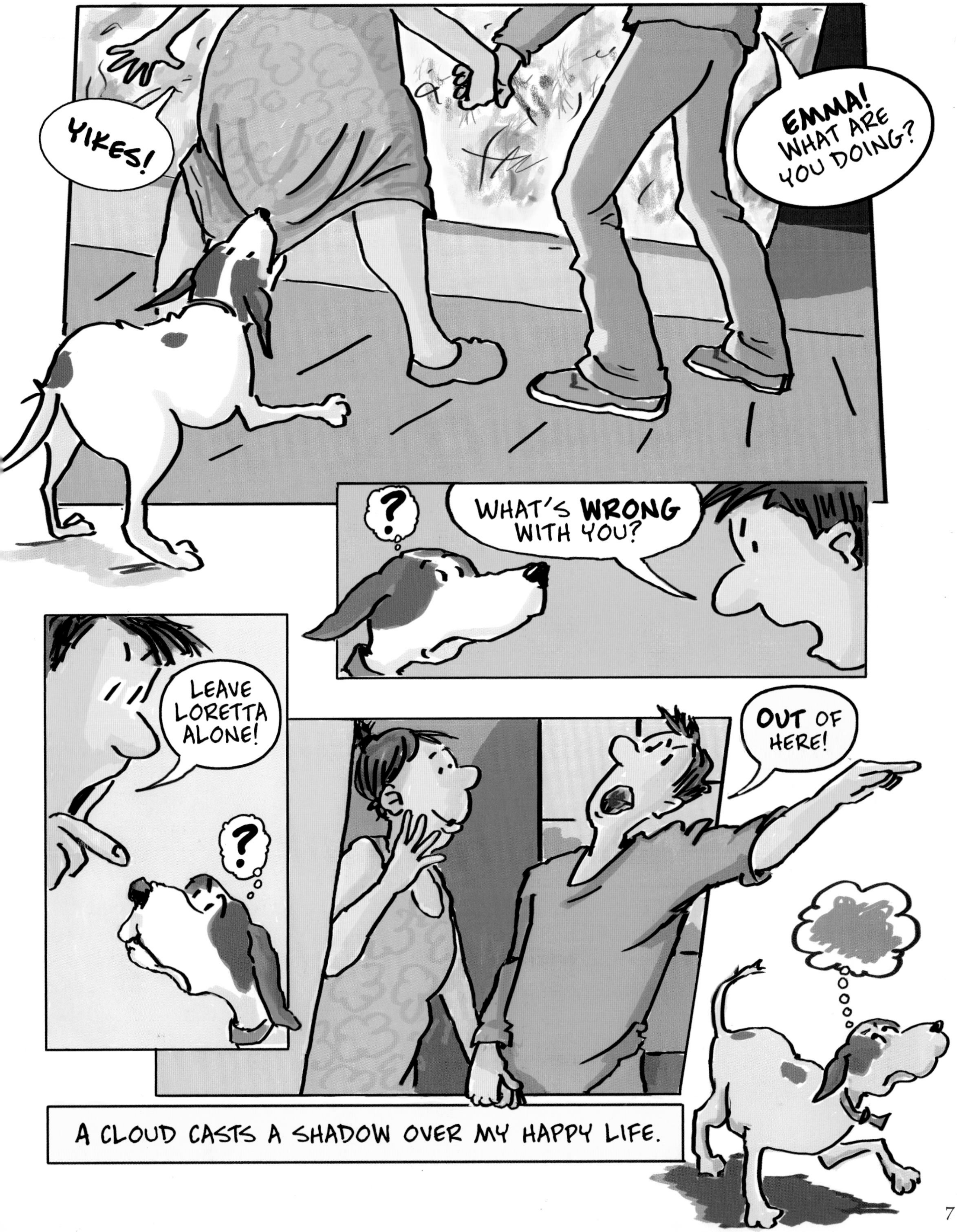
YIKES!
EMMA! WHAT ARE YOU DOING?
?
WHAT'S WRONG WITH YOU?
LEAVE LORETTA ALONE!
?
OUT OF HERE!
A CLOUD CASTS A SHADOW OVER MY HAPPY LIFE.

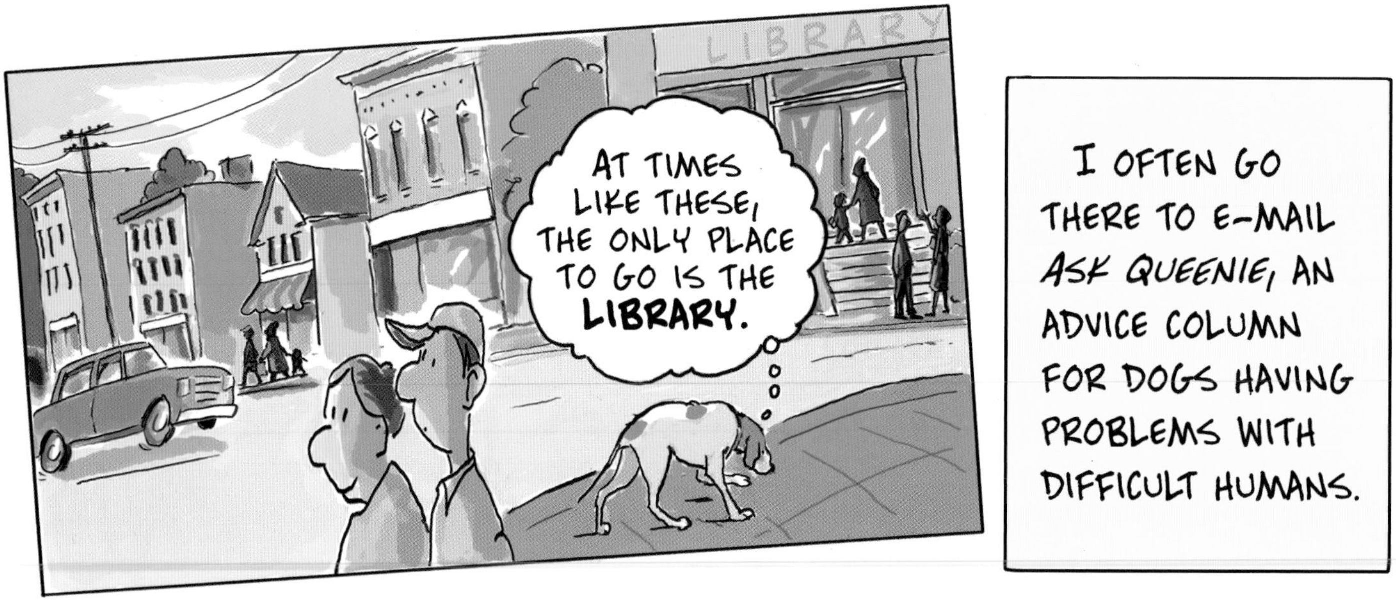
LIBRARY
AT TIMES LIKE THESE, THE ONLY PLACE TO GO IS THE **LIBRARY.**
I OFTEN GO THERE TO E-MAIL *ASK QUEENIE*, AN ADVICE COLUMN FOR DOGS HAVING PROBLEMS WITH DIFFICULT HUMANS.

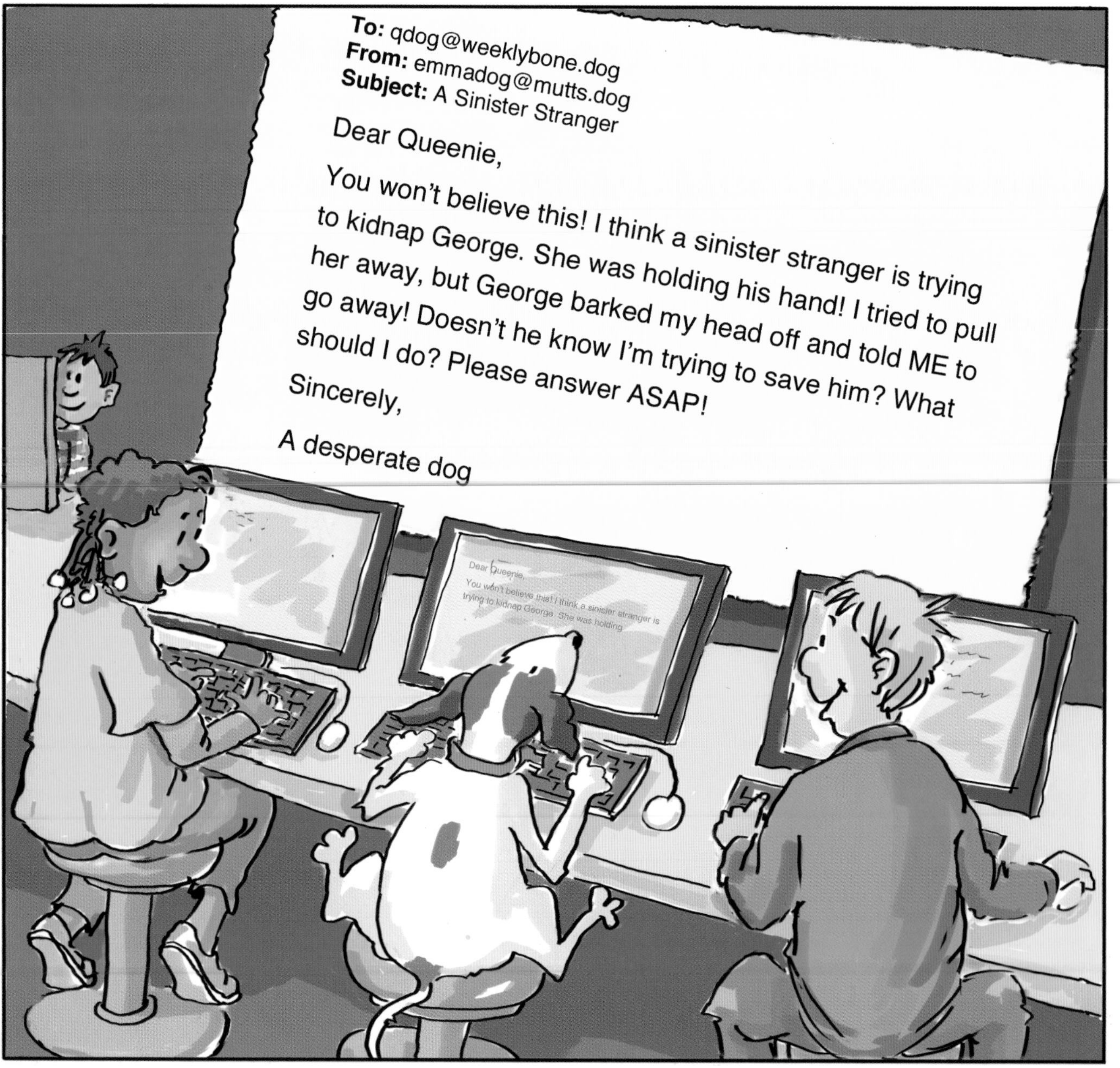
To: qdog@weeklybone.dog
From: emmadog@mutts.dog
Subject: A Sinister Stranger
Dear Queenie,
You won't believe this! I think a sinister stranger is trying to kidnap George. She was holding his hand! I tried to pull her away, but George barked my head off and told ME to go away! Doesn't he know I'm trying to save him? What should I do? Please answer ASAP!
Sincerely,
A desperate dog
Dear Queenie,
You won't believe this! I think a sinister stranger is trying to kidnap George. She was holding

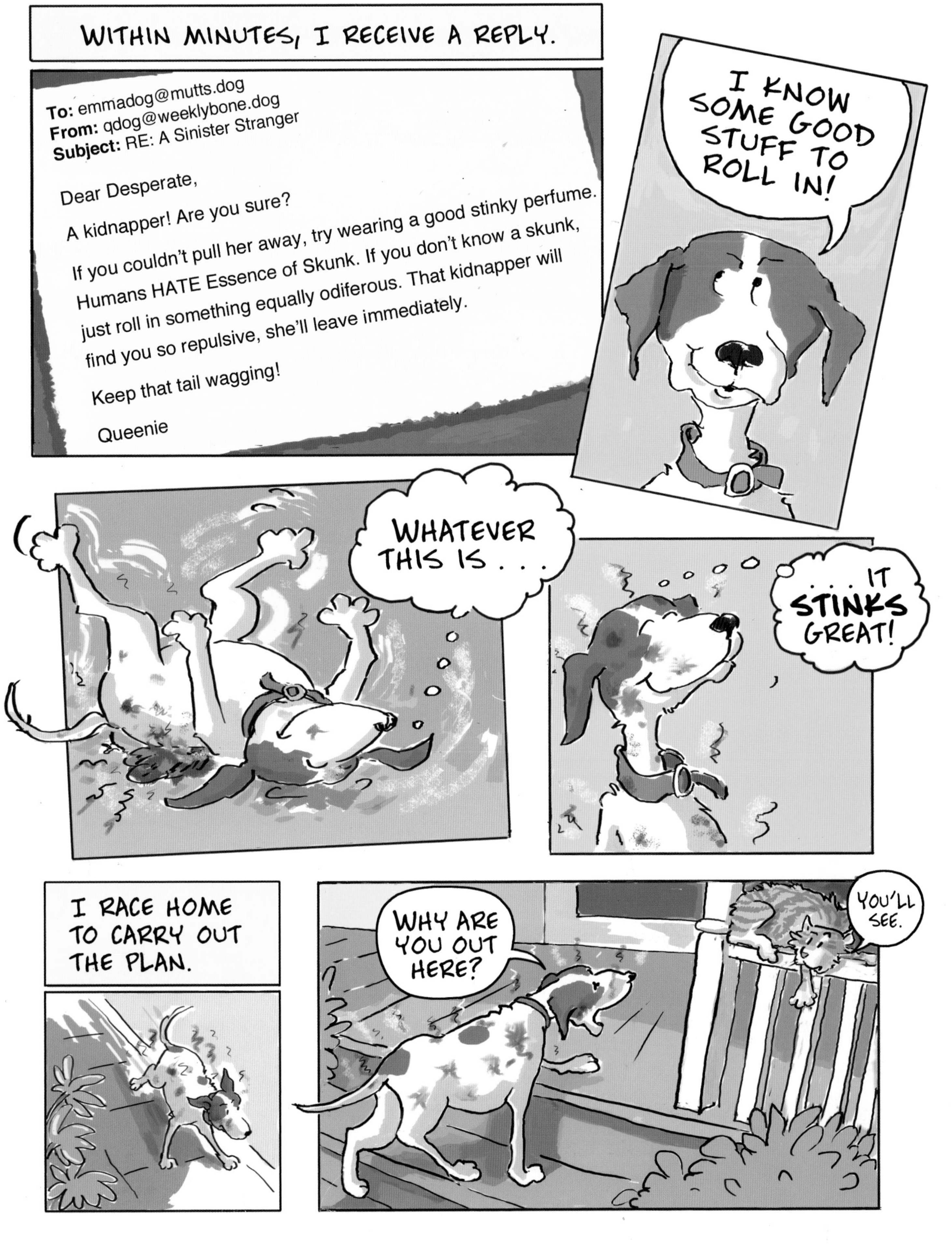
WITHIN MINUTES, I RECEIVE A REPLY.
To: emmadog@mutts.dog
From: qdog@weeklybone.dog
Subject: RE: A Sinister Stranger
Dear Desperate,
A kidnapper! Are you sure?
If you couldn't pull her away, try wearing a good stinky perfume. Humans HATE Essence of Skunk. If you don't know a skunk, just roll in something equally odiferous. That kidnapper will find you so repulsive, she'll leave immediately.
Keep that tail wagging!
Queenie
I KNOW SOME GOOD STUFF TO ROLL IN!
WHATEVER THIS IS . . .
. . . IT STINKS GREAT!
I RACE HOME TO CARRY OUT THE PLAN.
WHY ARE YOU OUT HERE?
YOU'LL SEE.

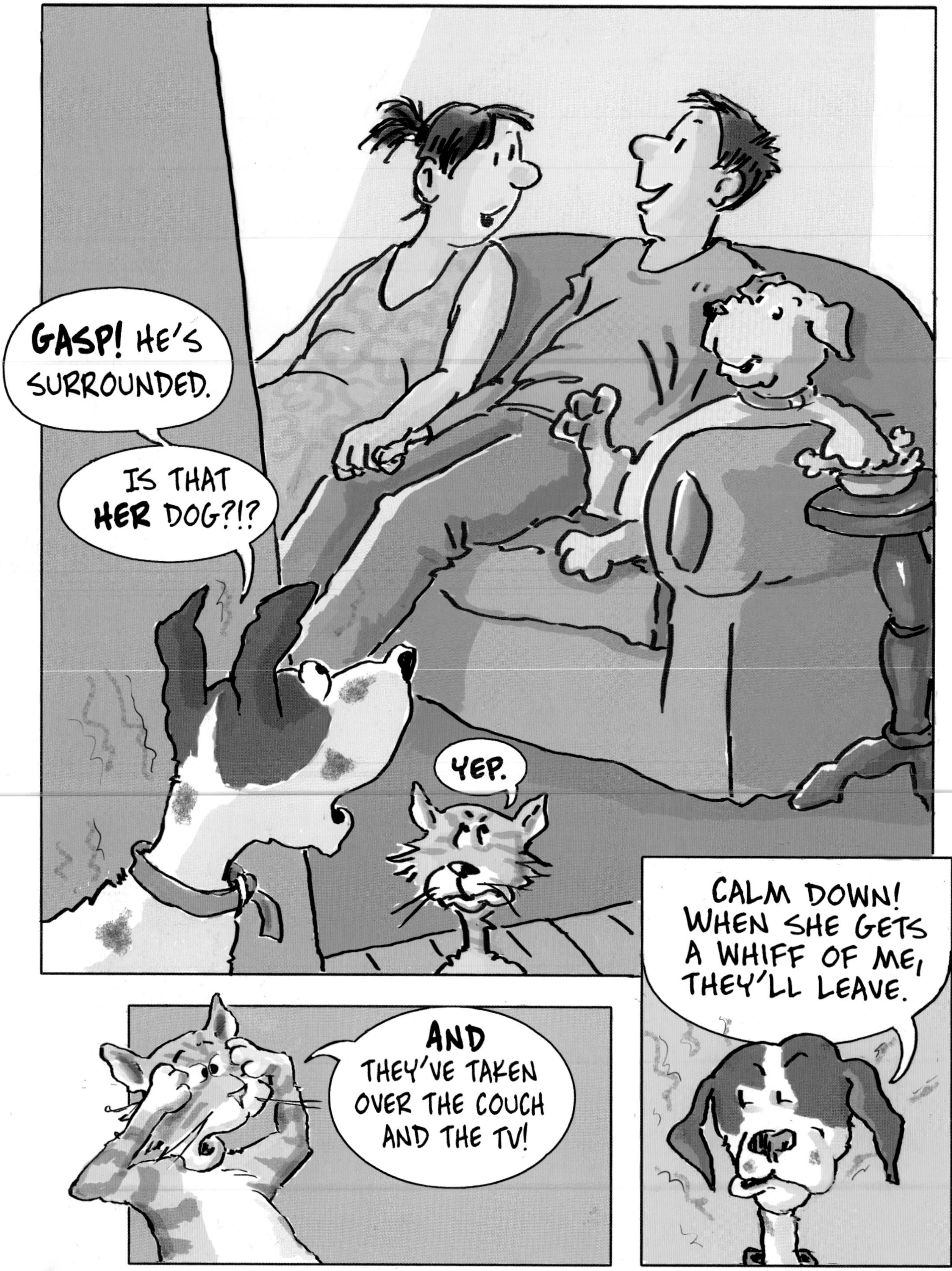
GASP! HE'S SURROUNDED.
IS THAT HER DOG?!?
YEP.
AND THEY'VE TAKEN OVER THE COUCH AND THE TV!
CALM DOWN! WHEN SHE GETS A WHIFF OF ME, THEY'LL LEAVE.

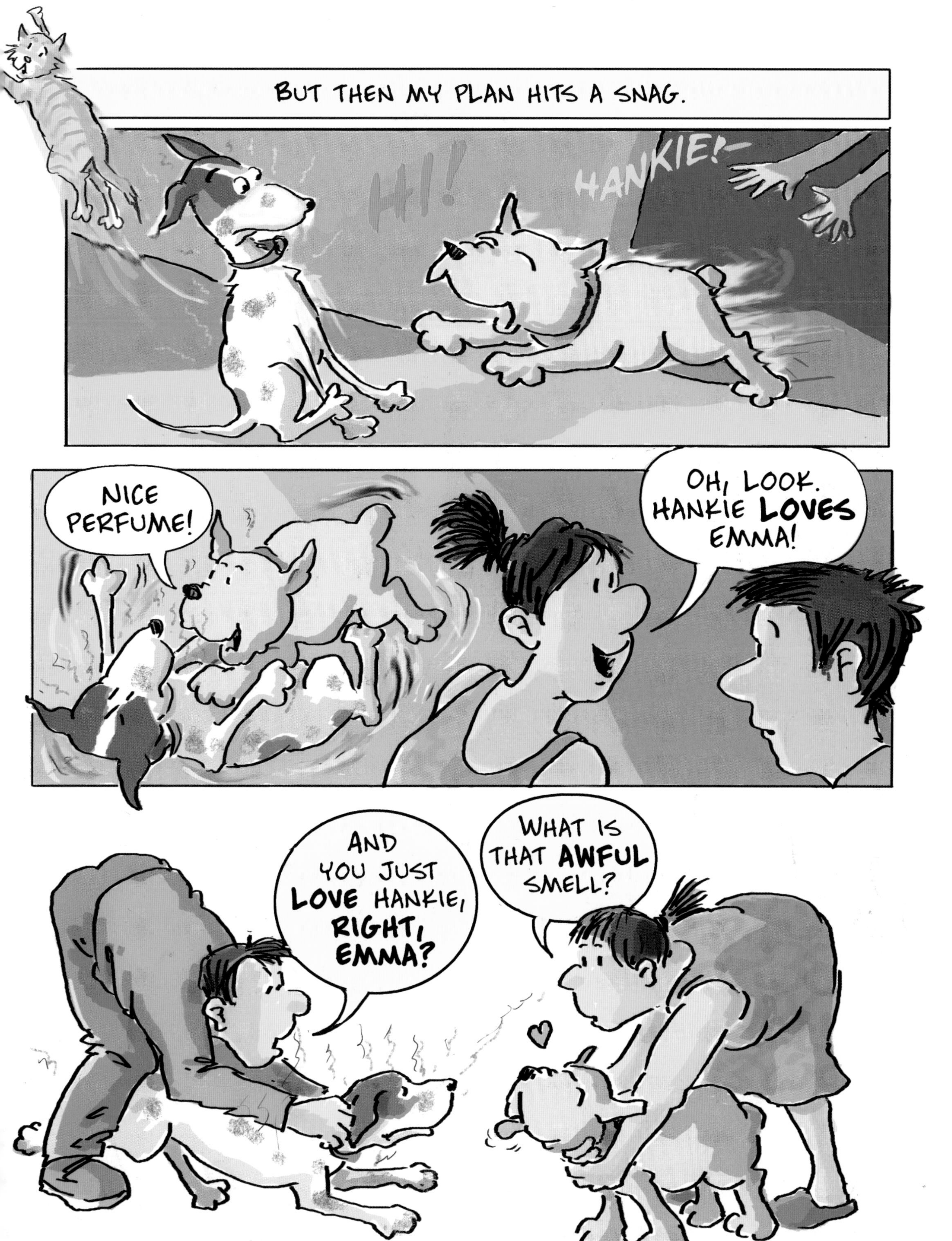
BUT THEN MY PLAN HITS A SNAG.
HI!
HANKIE!
NICE PERFUME!
OH, LOOK. HANKIE LOVES EMMA!
AND YOU JUST LOVE HANKIE, RIGHT, EMMA?
WHAT IS THAT AWFUL SMELL?

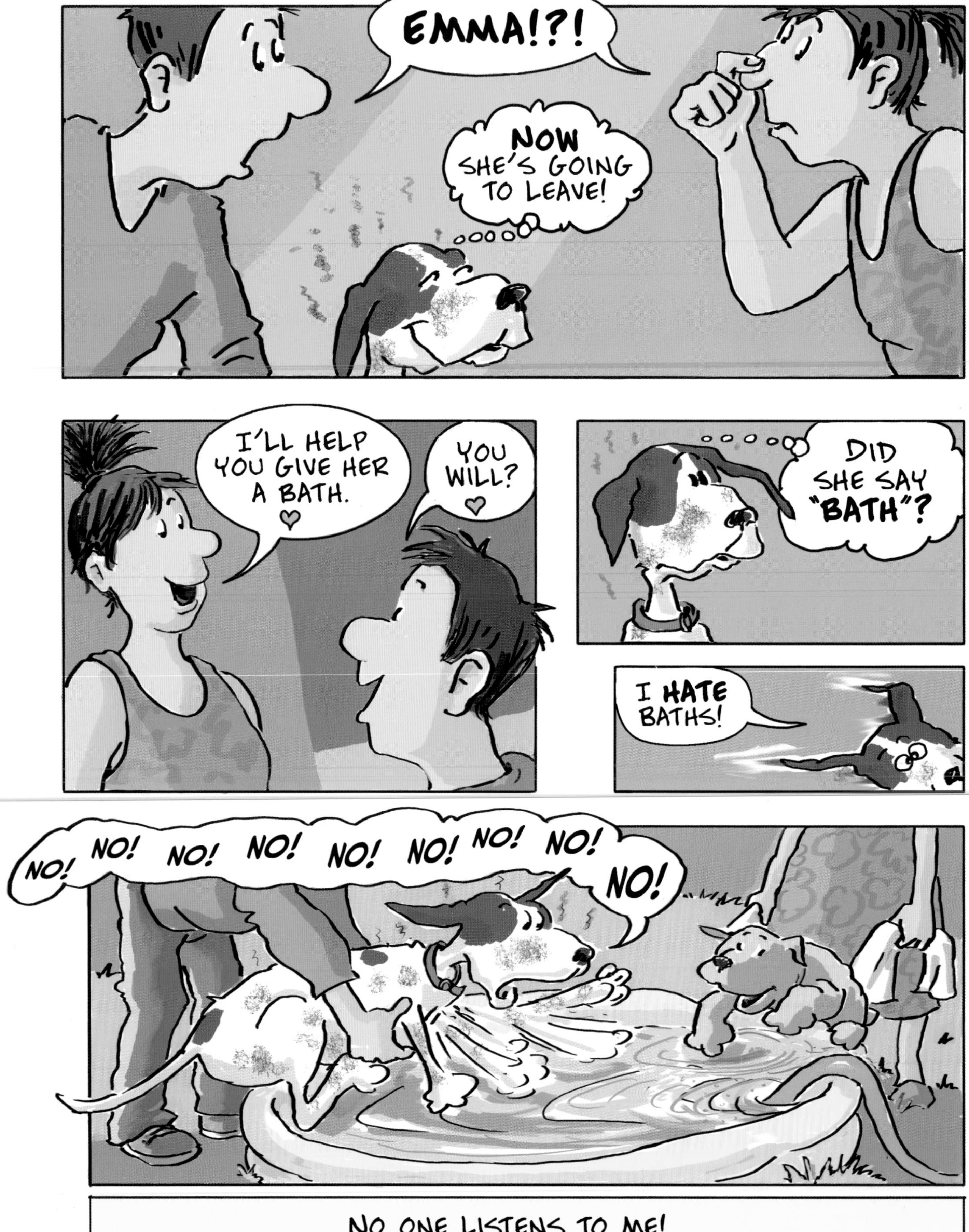
EMMA!?!
NOW SHE'S GOING TO LEAVE!
I'LL HELP YOU GIVE HER A BATH.
YOU WILL?
DID SHE SAY "BATH"?
I HATE BATHS!
NO! NO! NO! NO! NO! NO! NO! NO! NO!
NO ONE LISTENS TO ME!

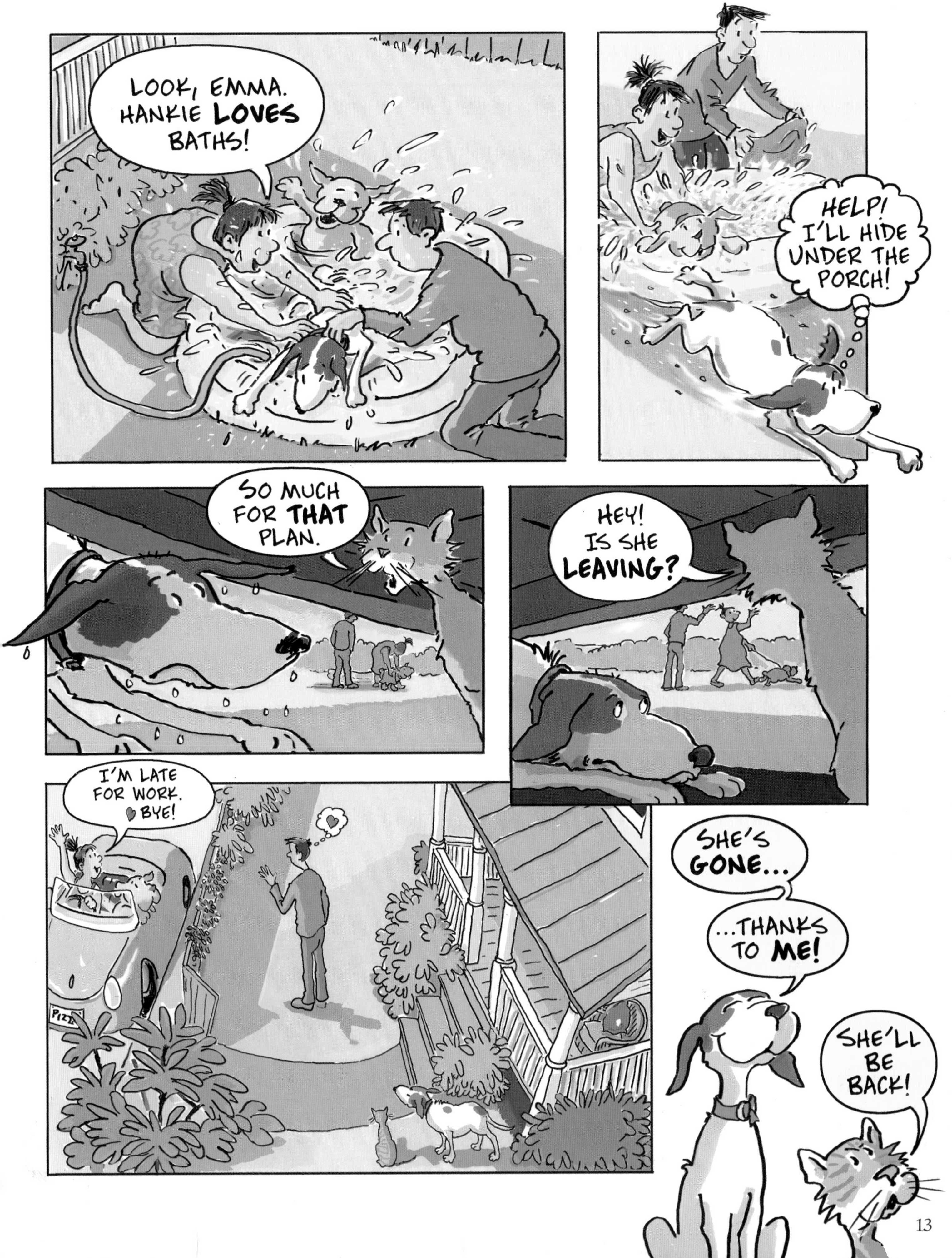
LOOK, EMMA. HANKIE **LOVES** BATHS!
HELP! I'LL HIDE UNDER THE PORCH!
SO MUCH FOR **THAT** PLAN.
HEY! IS SHE **LEAVING**?
I'M LATE FOR WORK. ♥ BYE!
PIZZ
SHE'S **GONE...**
...THANKS TO **ME!**
SHE'LL BE BACK!

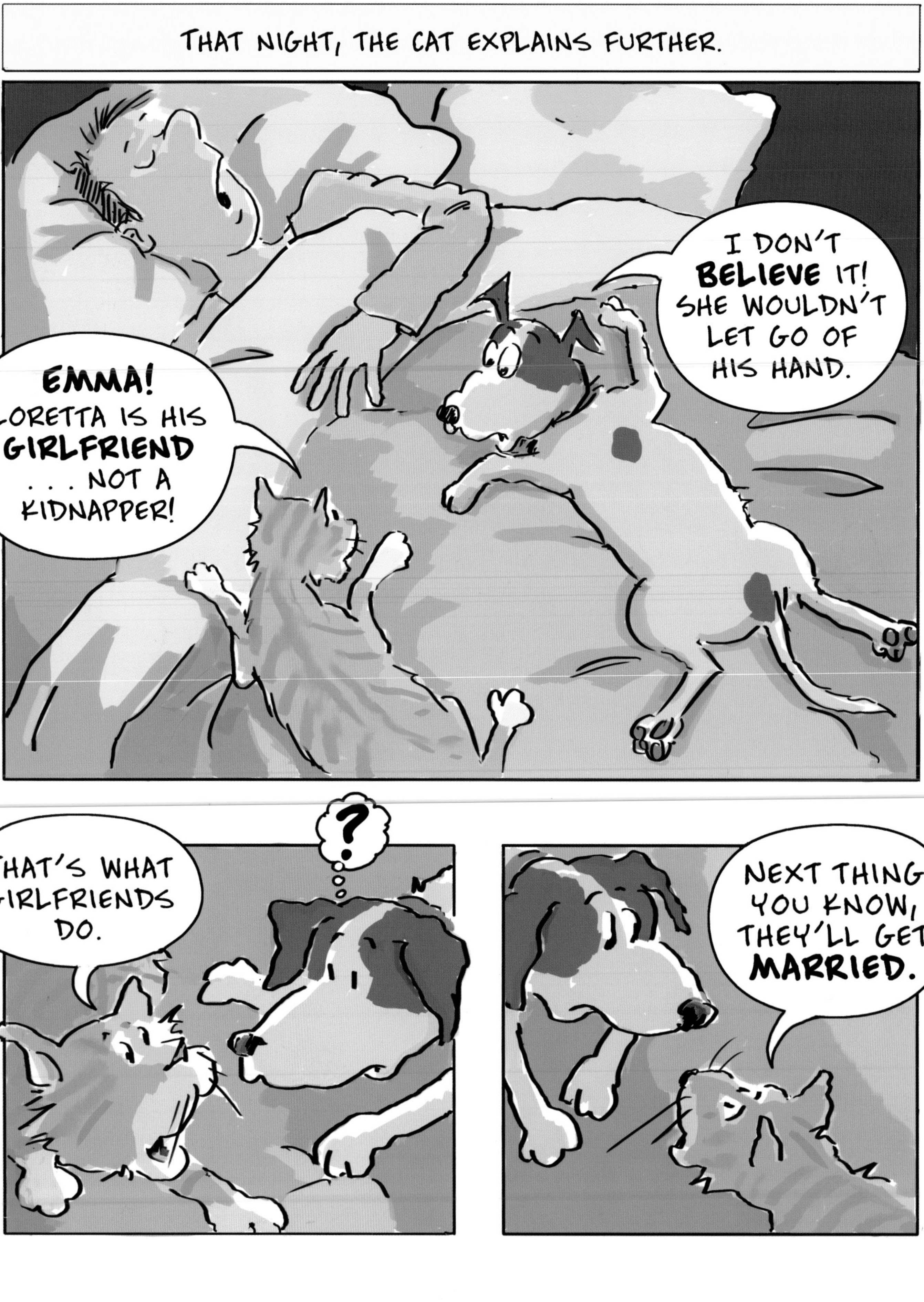
THAT NIGHT, THE CAT EXPLAINS FURTHER.
I DON'T BELIEVE IT! SHE WOULDN'T LET GO OF HIS HAND.
EMMA! LORETTA IS HIS GIRLFRIEND . . . NOT A KIDNAPPER!
THAT'S WHAT GIRLFRIENDS DO.
?
NEXT THING YOU KNOW, THEY'LL GET MARRIED.

THE CAT'S REVELATION IS SO DISTRESSING, I CONTACT QUEENIE IMMEDIATELY. I BORROW GEORGE'S COMPUTER.

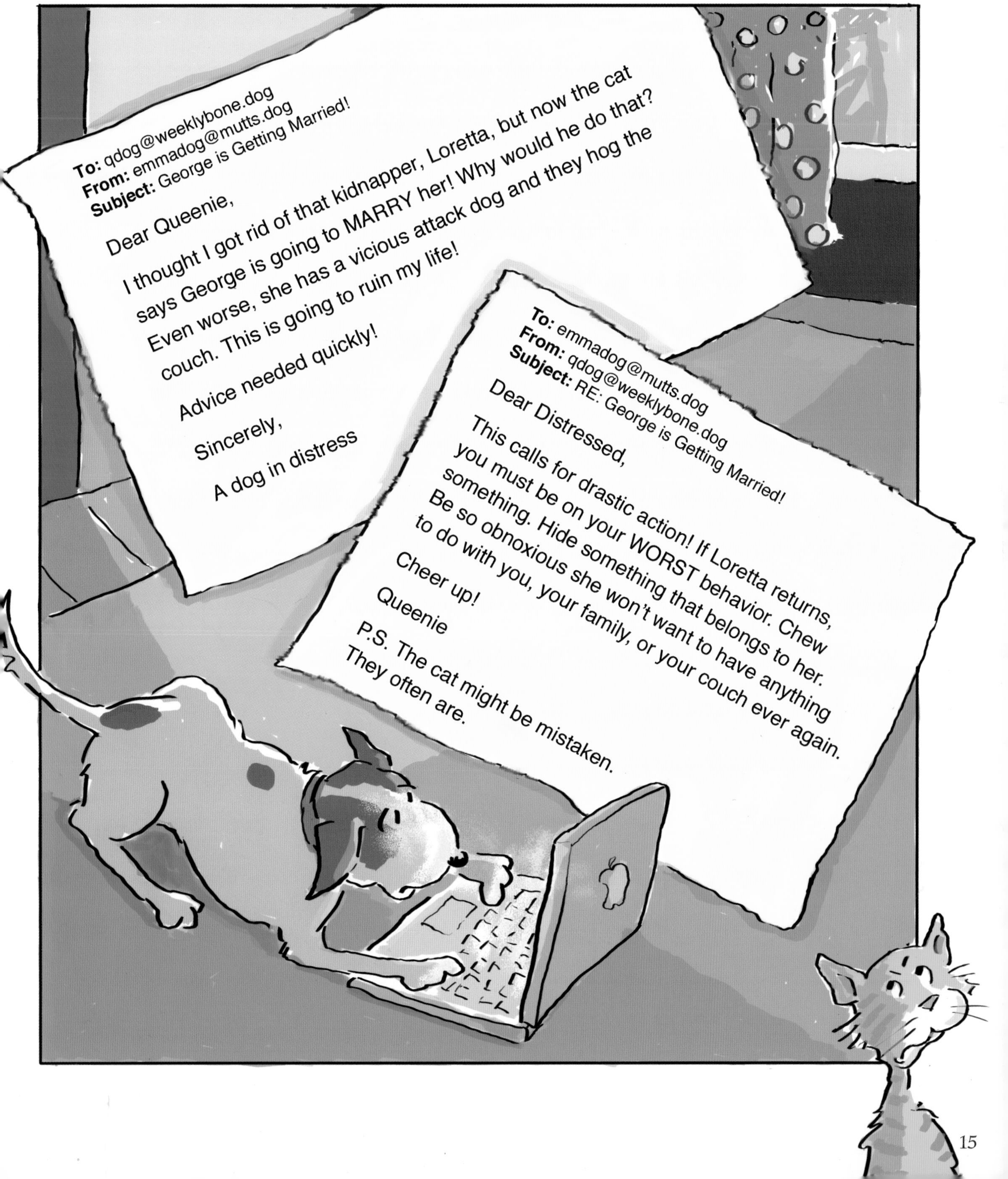
To: qdog@weeklybone.dog
From: emmadog@mutts.dog
Subject: George is Getting Married!
Dear Queenie,
I thought I got rid of that kidnapper, Loretta, but now the cat says George is going to MARRY her! Why would he do that? Even worse, she has a vicious attack dog and they hog the couch. This is going to ruin my life!
Advice needed quickly!
Sincerely,
A dog in distress
To: emmadog@mutts.dog
From: qdog@weeklybone.dog
Subject: RE: George is Getting Married!
Dear Distressed,
This calls for drastic action! If Loretta returns, you must be on your WORST behavior. Chew something. Hide something that belongs to her. Be so obnoxious she won't want to have anything to do with you, your family, or your couch ever again.
Cheer up!
Queenie
P.S. The cat might be mistaken. They often are.

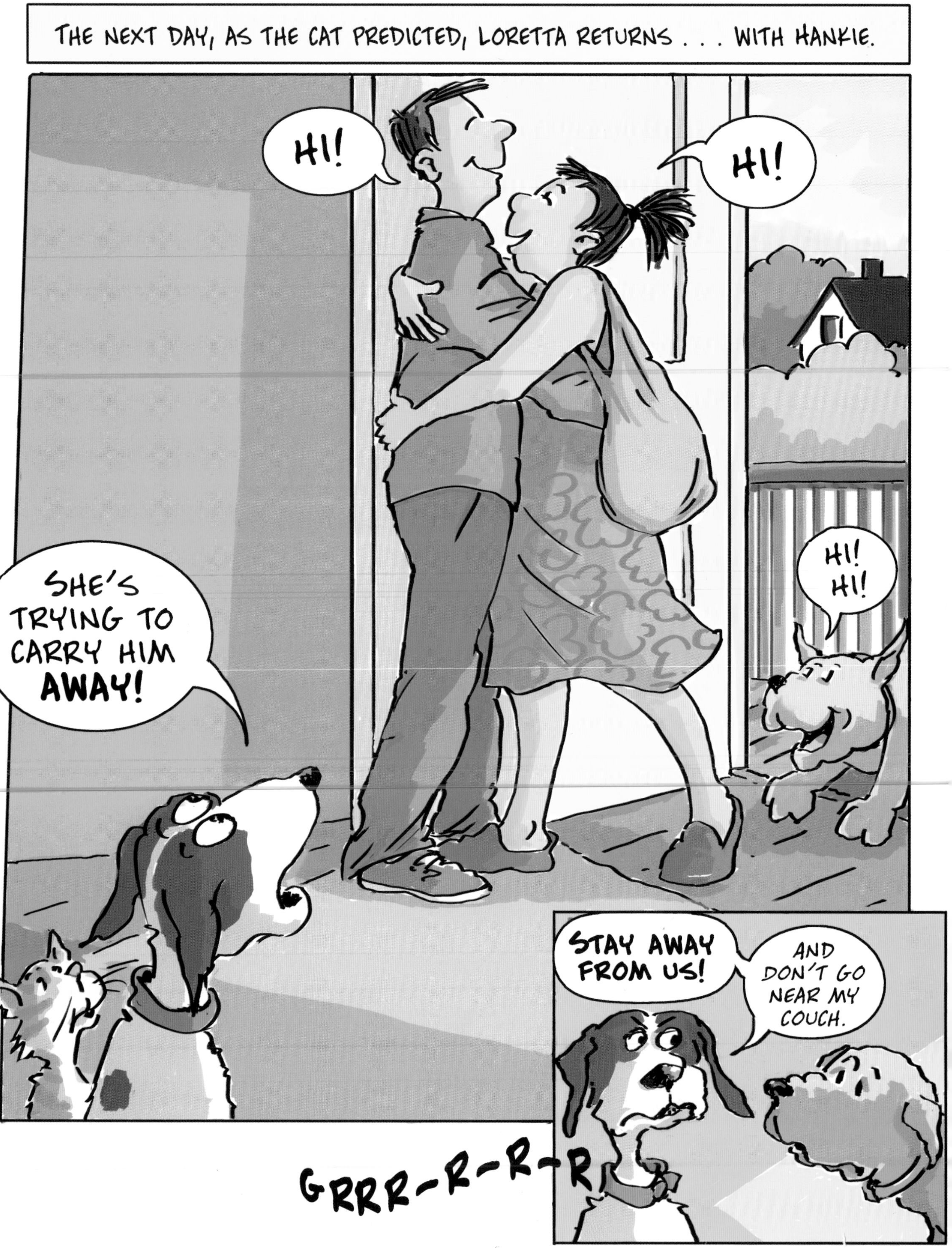
THE NEXT DAY, AS THE CAT PREDICTED, LORETTA RETURNS . . . WITH HANKIE.
HI!
HI!
HI! HI!
SHE'S TRYING TO CARRY HIM **AWAY!**
STAY AWAY FROM US!
AND DON'T GO NEAR MY COUCH.
GRRR-R-R-R

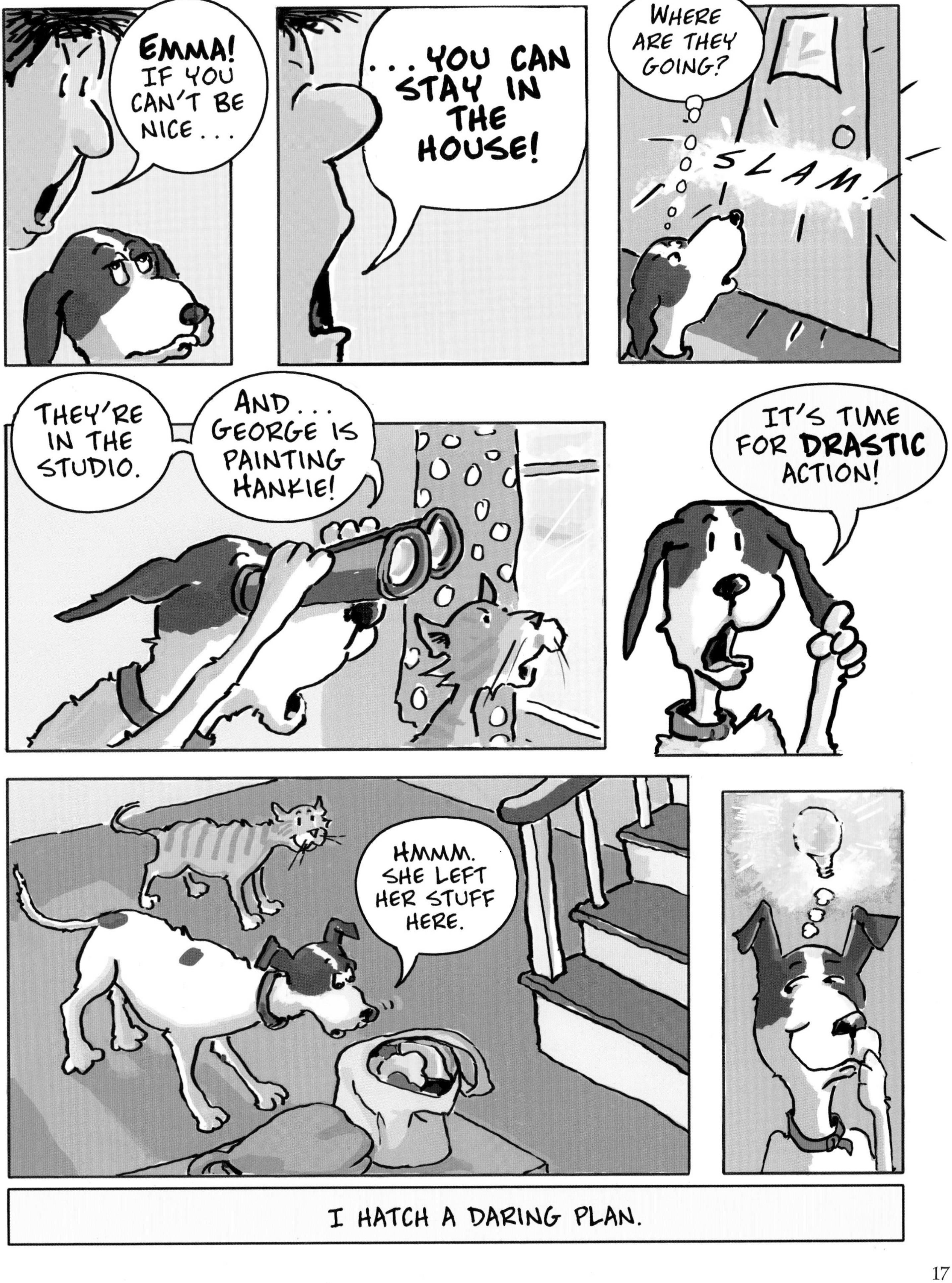
EMMA! IF YOU CAN'T BE NICE . . .
. . . YOU CAN STAY IN THE HOUSE!
WHERE ARE THEY GOING?
SLAM!
THEY'RE IN THE STUDIO.
AND . . . GEORGE IS PAINTING HANKIE!
IT'S TIME FOR DRASTIC ACTION!
HMMM. SHE LEFT HER STUFF HERE.
I HATCH A DARING PLAN.

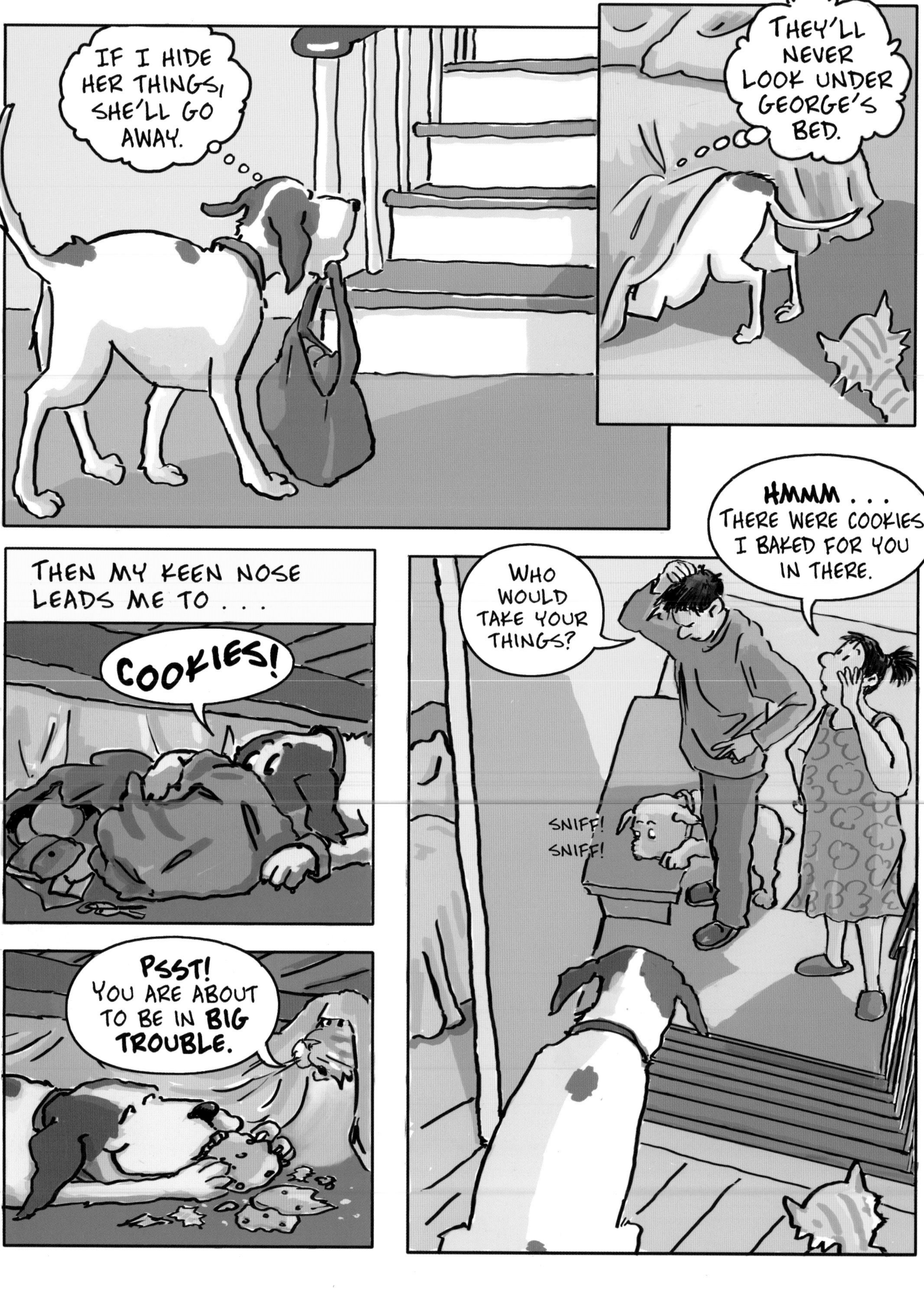
IF I HIDE HER THINGS, SHE'LL GO AWAY.
THEY'LL NEVER LOOK UNDER GEORGE'S BED.
THEN MY KEEN NOSE LEADS ME TO . . .
COOKIES!
PSST! YOU ARE ABOUT TO BE IN BIG TROUBLE.
HMMM . . . THERE WERE COOKIES I BAKED FOR YOU IN THERE.
WHO WOULD TAKE YOUR THINGS?
SNIFF! SNIFF!

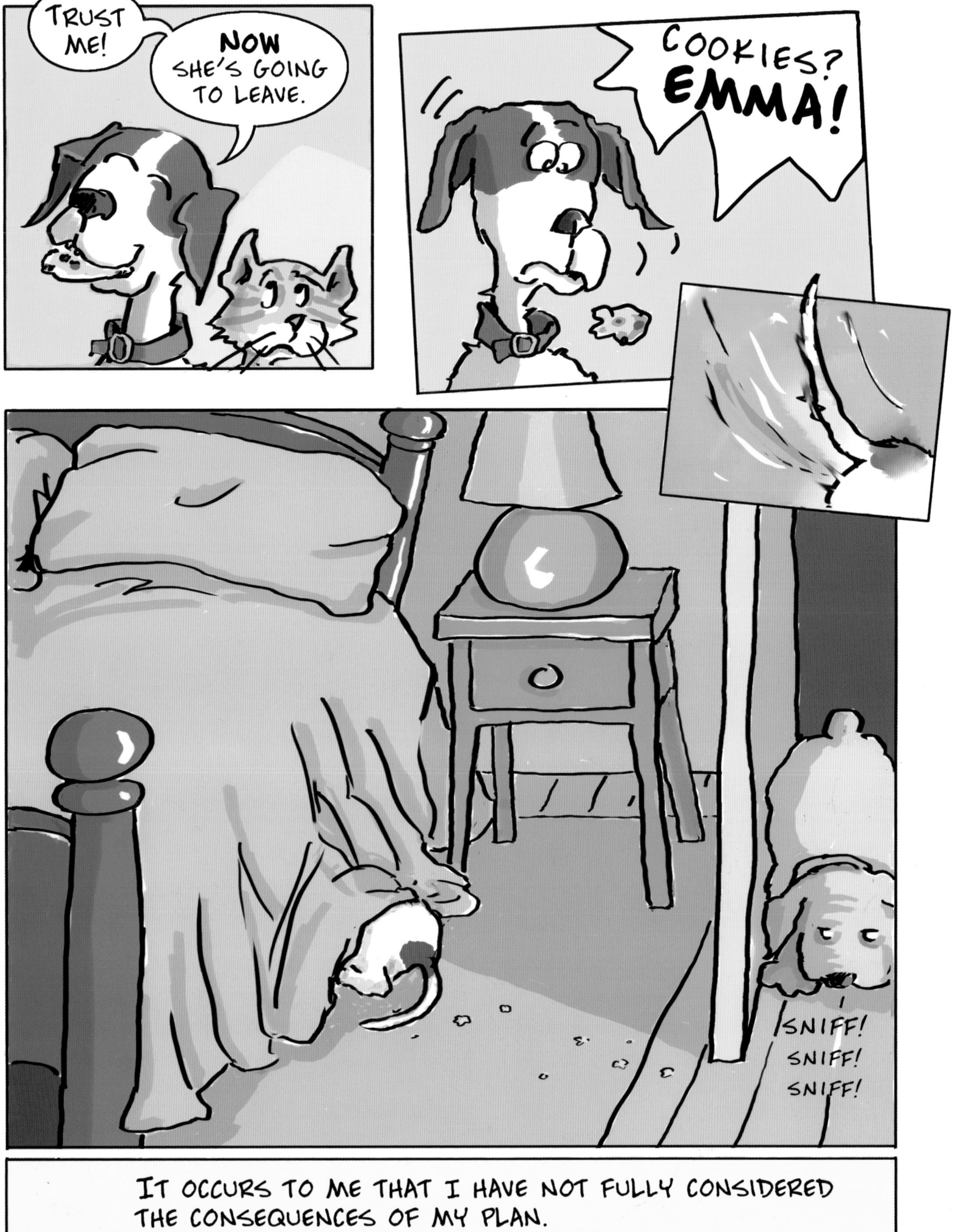
TRUST ME!
NOW SHE'S GOING TO LEAVE.
COOKIES? EMMA!
SNIFF! SNIFF! SNIFF!
IT OCCURS TO ME THAT I HAVE NOT FULLY CONSIDERED THE CONSEQUENCES OF MY PLAN.

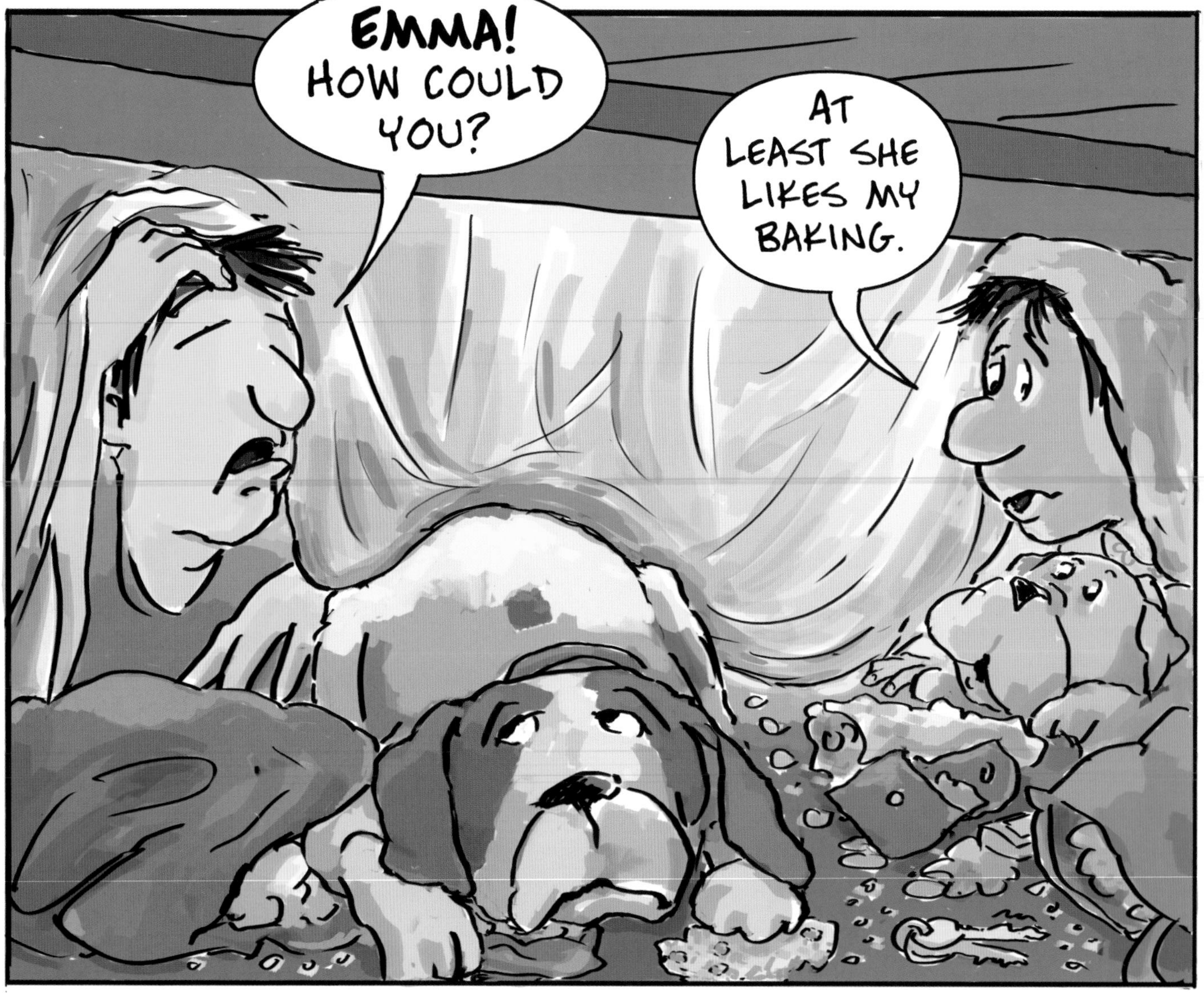
EMMA! HOW COULD YOU?
AT LEAST SHE LIKES MY BAKING.

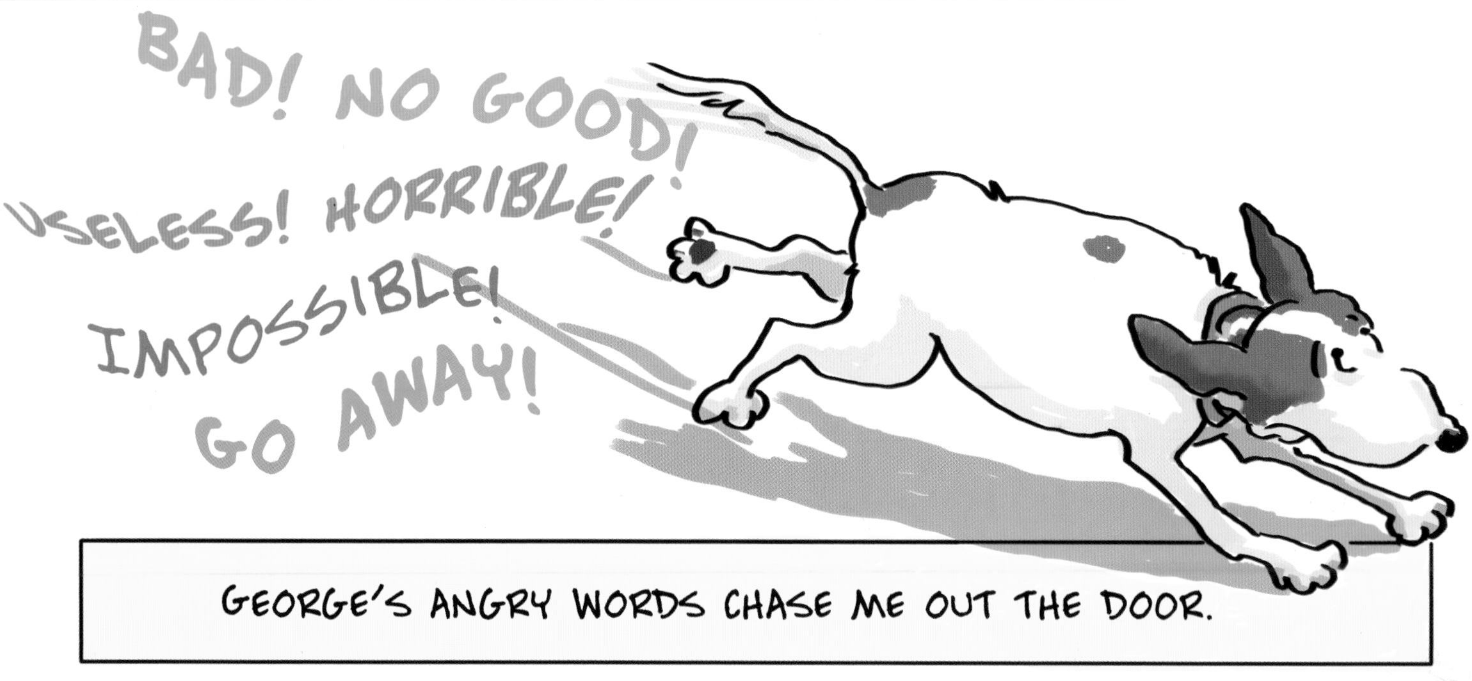
BAD! NO GOOD!
USELESS! HORRIBLE!
IMPOSSIBLE!
GO AWAY!
GEORGE'S ANGRY WORDS CHASE ME OUT THE DOOR.

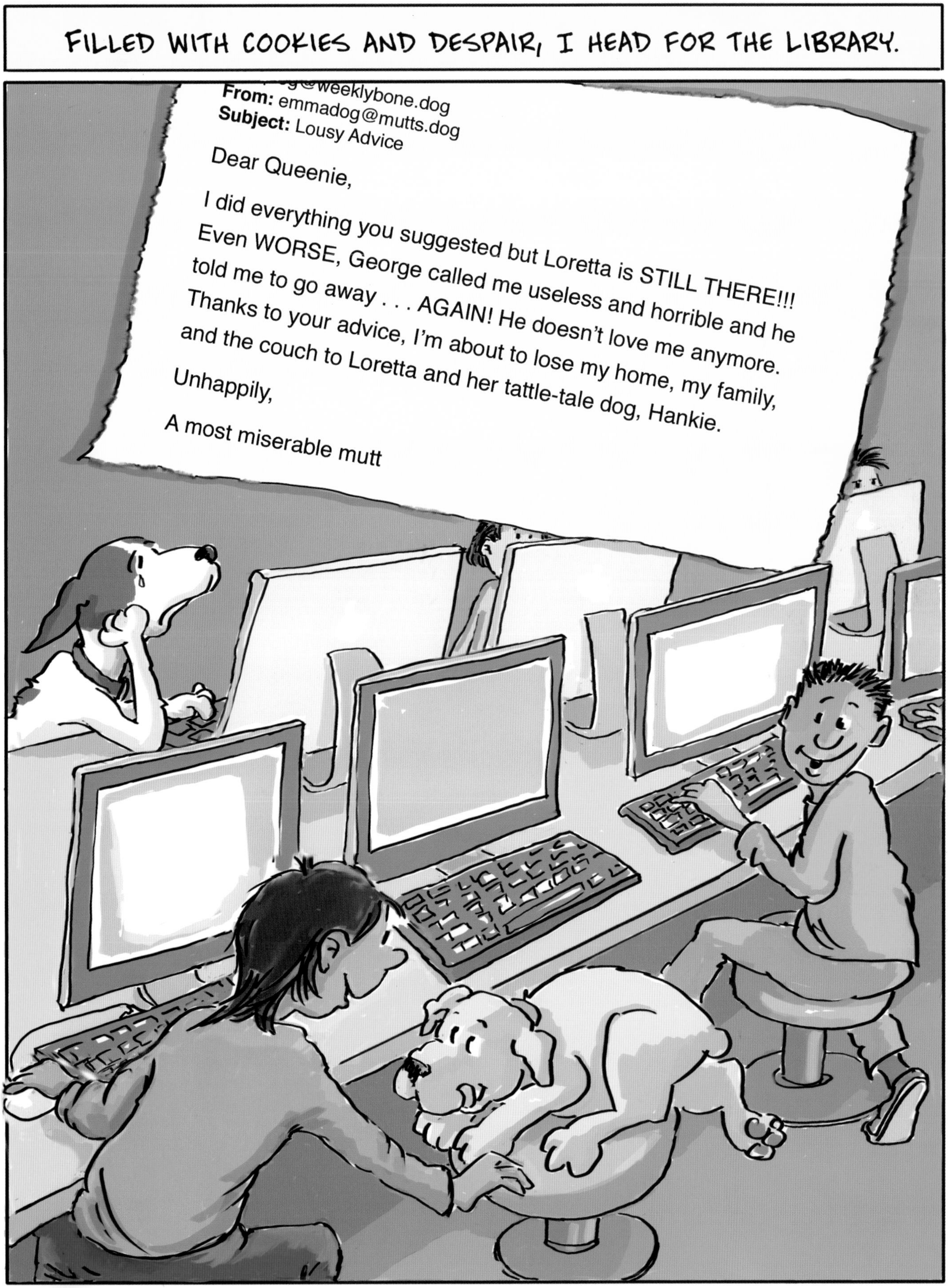
FILLED WITH COOKIES AND DESPAIR, I HEAD FOR THE LIBRARY.
From: emmadog@mutts.dog
Subject: Lousy Advice
Dear Queenie,
I did everything you suggested but Loretta is STILL THERE!!! Even WORSE, George called me useless and horrible and he told me to go away . . . AGAIN! He doesn't love me anymore. Thanks to your advice, I'm about to lose my home, my family, and the couch to Loretta and her tattle-tale dog, Hankie.
Unhappily,
A most miserable mutt

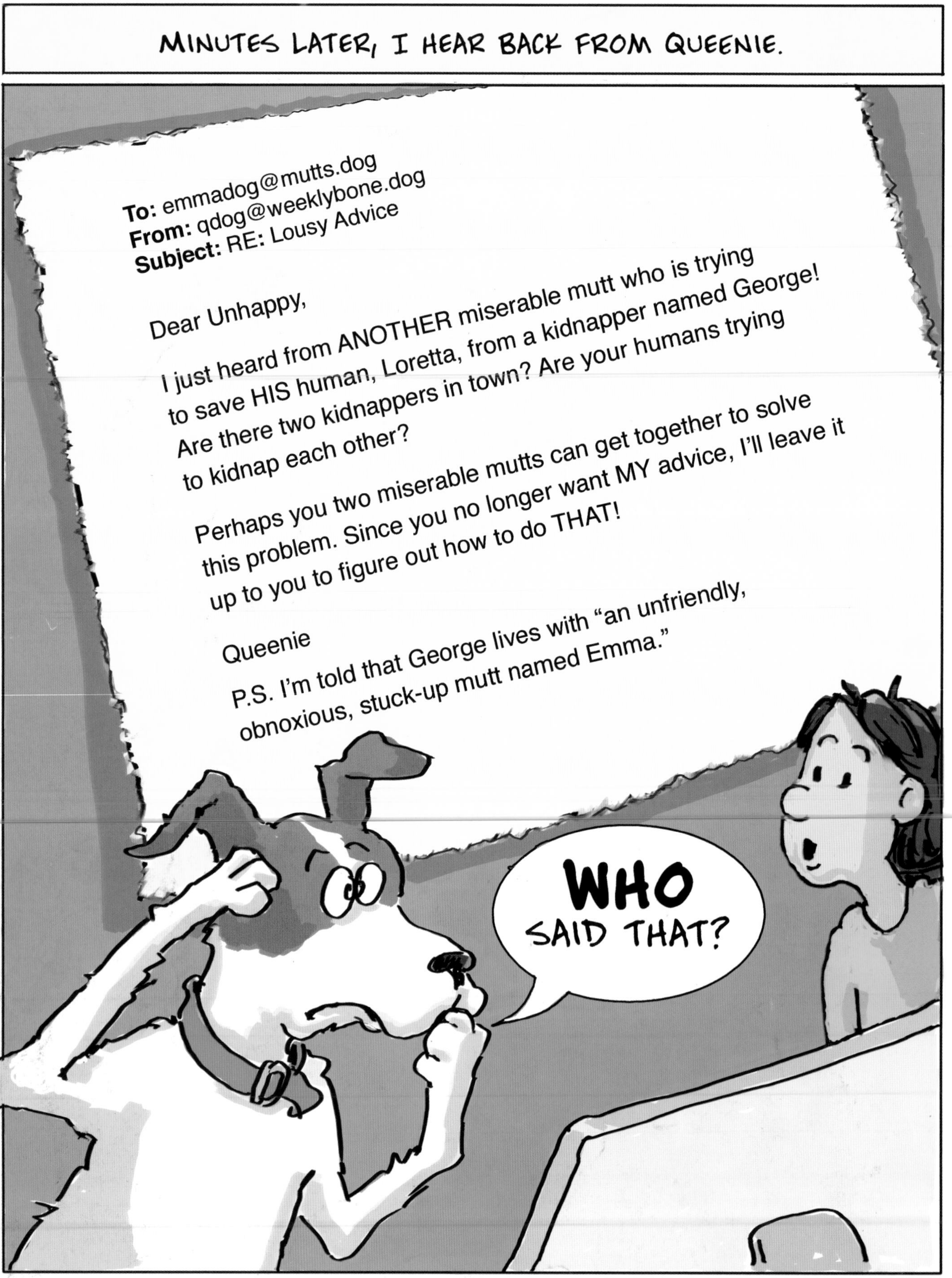
MINUTES LATER, I HEAR BACK FROM QUEENIE.
To: emmadog@mutts.dog
From: qdog@weeklybone.dog
Subject: RE: Lousy Advice
Dear Unhappy,
I just heard from ANOTHER miserable mutt who is trying to save HIS human, Loretta, from a kidnapper named George! Are there two kidnappers in town? Are your humans trying to kidnap each other?
Perhaps you two miserable mutts can get together to solve this problem. Since you no longer want MY advice, I'll leave it up to you to figure out how to do THAT!
Queenie
P.S. I'm told that George lives with "an unfriendly, obnoxious, stuck-up mutt named Emma."
WHO SAID THAT?

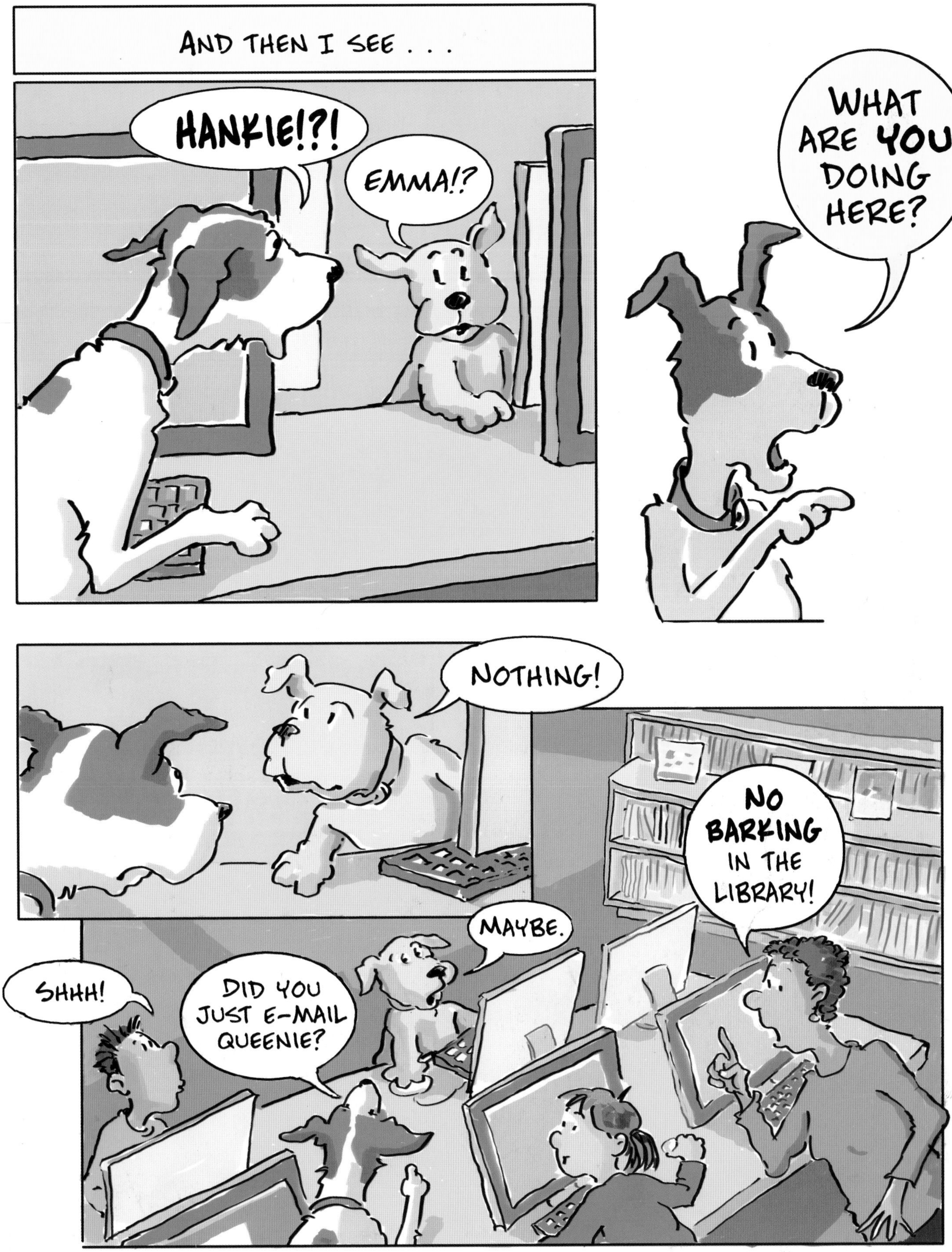
AND THEN I SEE . . .
HANKIE!?!
EMMA!?
WHAT ARE YOU DOING HERE?
NOTHING!
NO BARKING IN THE LIBRARY!
MAYBE.
SHHH!
DID YOU JUST E-MAIL QUEENIE?

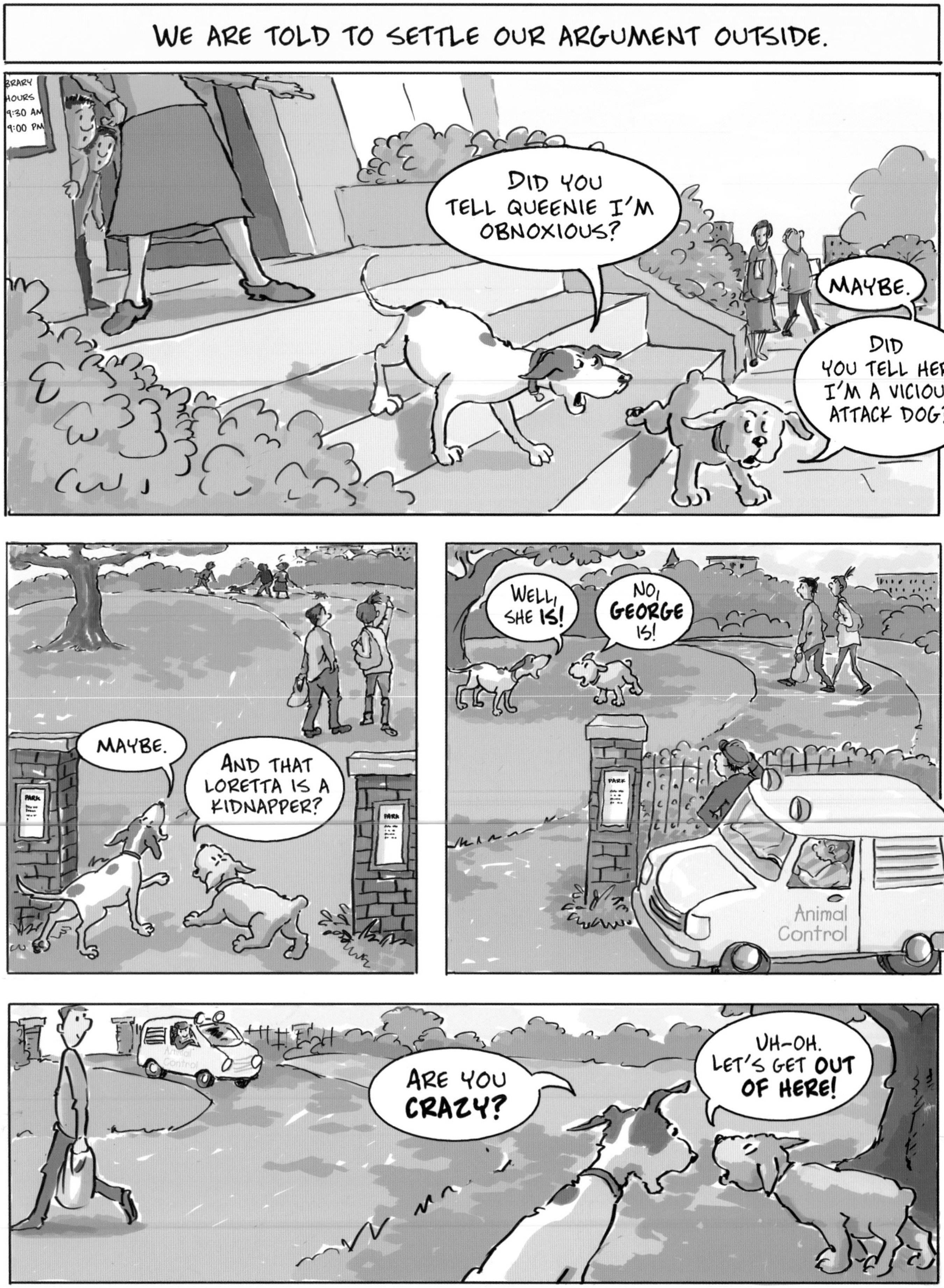
WE ARE TOLD TO SETTLE OUR ARGUMENT OUTSIDE.
BRARY HOURS 9:30 AM 9:00 PM
DID YOU TELL QUEENIE I'M OBNOXIOUS?
MAYBE.
DID YOU TELL HER I'M A VICIOUS ATTACK DOG?
MAYBE.
AND THAT LORETTA IS A KIDNAPPER?
PARK
PARK
WELL, SHE IS!
NO, GEORGE IS!
PARK
Animal Control
ARE YOU CRAZY?
UH-OH. LET'S GET OUT OF HERE!

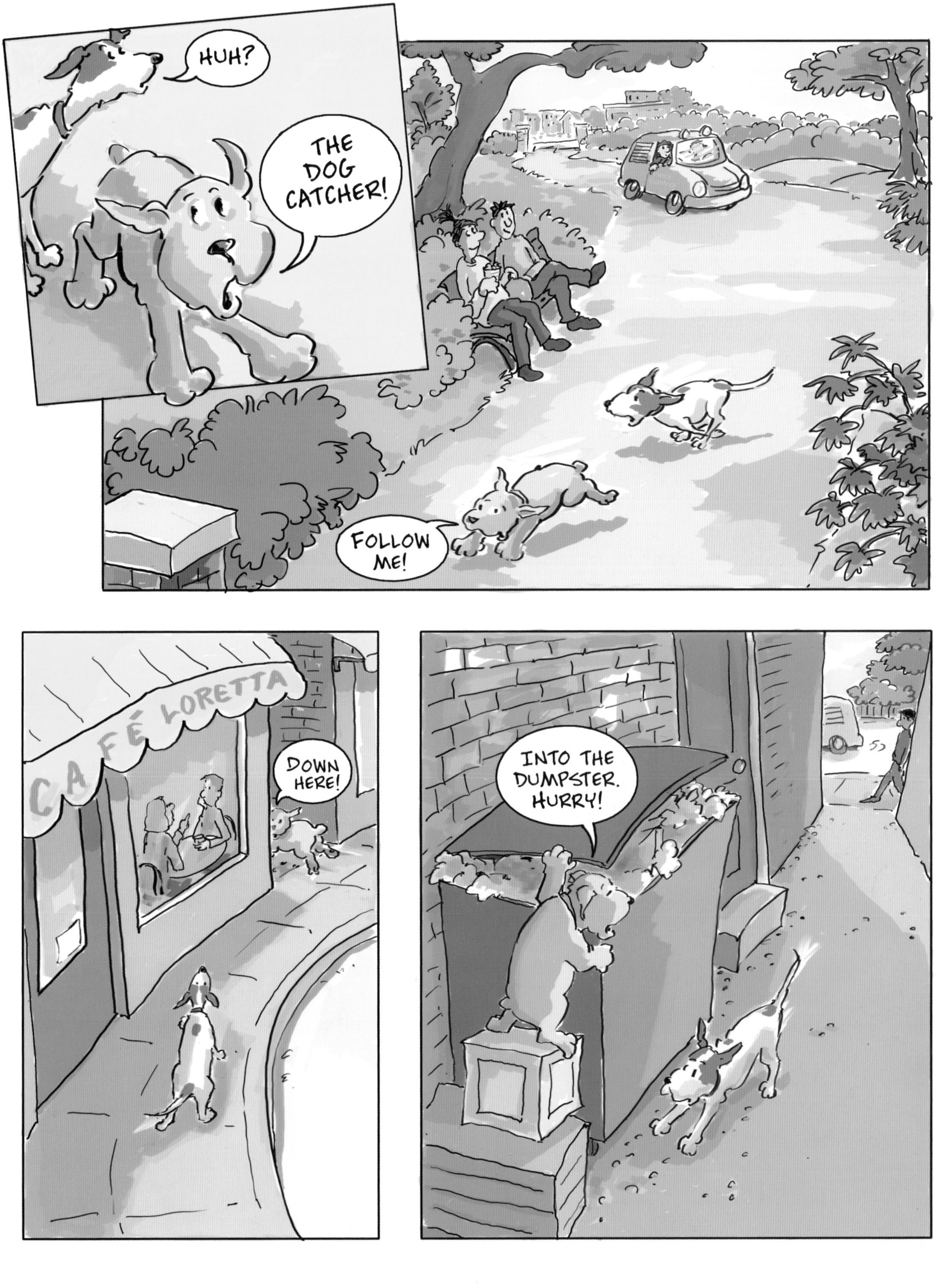
HUH?
THE DOG CATCHER!
FOLLOW ME!
CAFÉ LORETTA
DOWN HERE!
INTO THE DUMPSTER. HURRY!

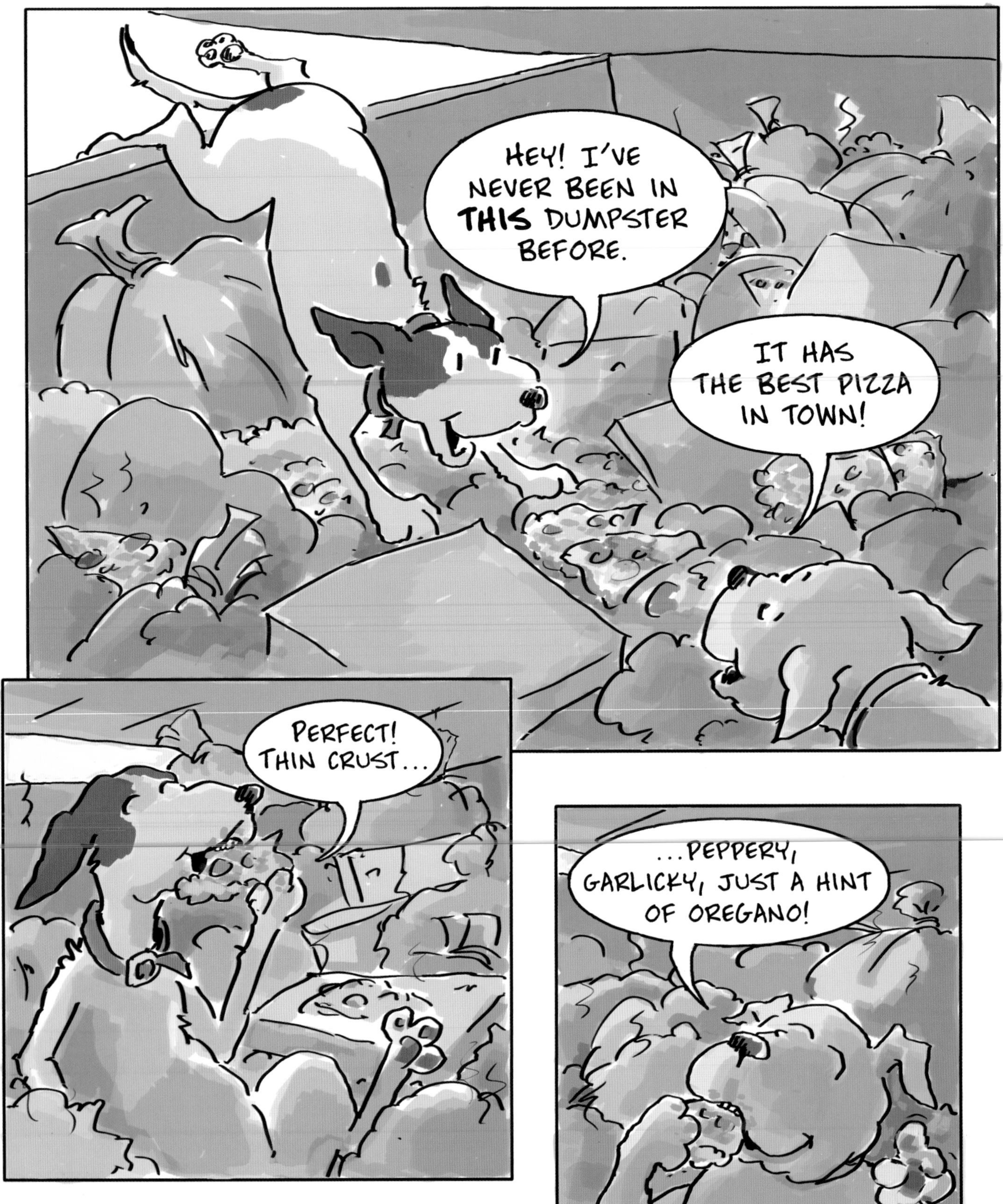
HEY! I'VE NEVER BEEN IN THIS DUMPSTER BEFORE.
IT HAS THE BEST PIZZA IN TOWN!
PERFECT! THIN CRUST...
...PEPPERY, GARLICKY, JUST A HINT OF OREGANO!
AT THIS MOMENT I REALIZE HANKIE AND I HAVE A LOT IN COMMON.

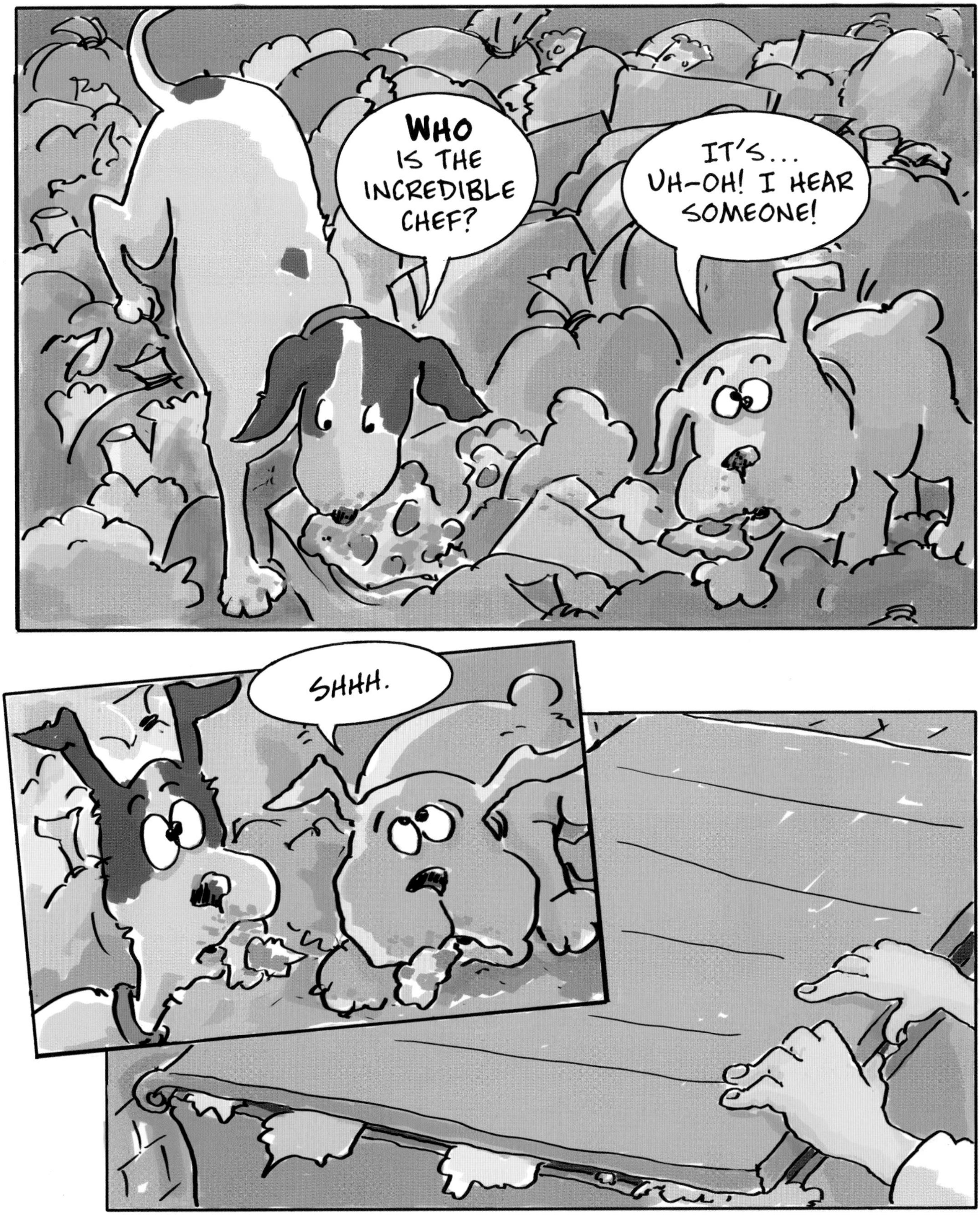
WHO IS THE INCREDIBLE CHEF?
IT'S... UH-OH! I HEAR SOMEONE!
SHHH.
YOU WILL NEVER GUESS WHAT HAPPENS NEXT!

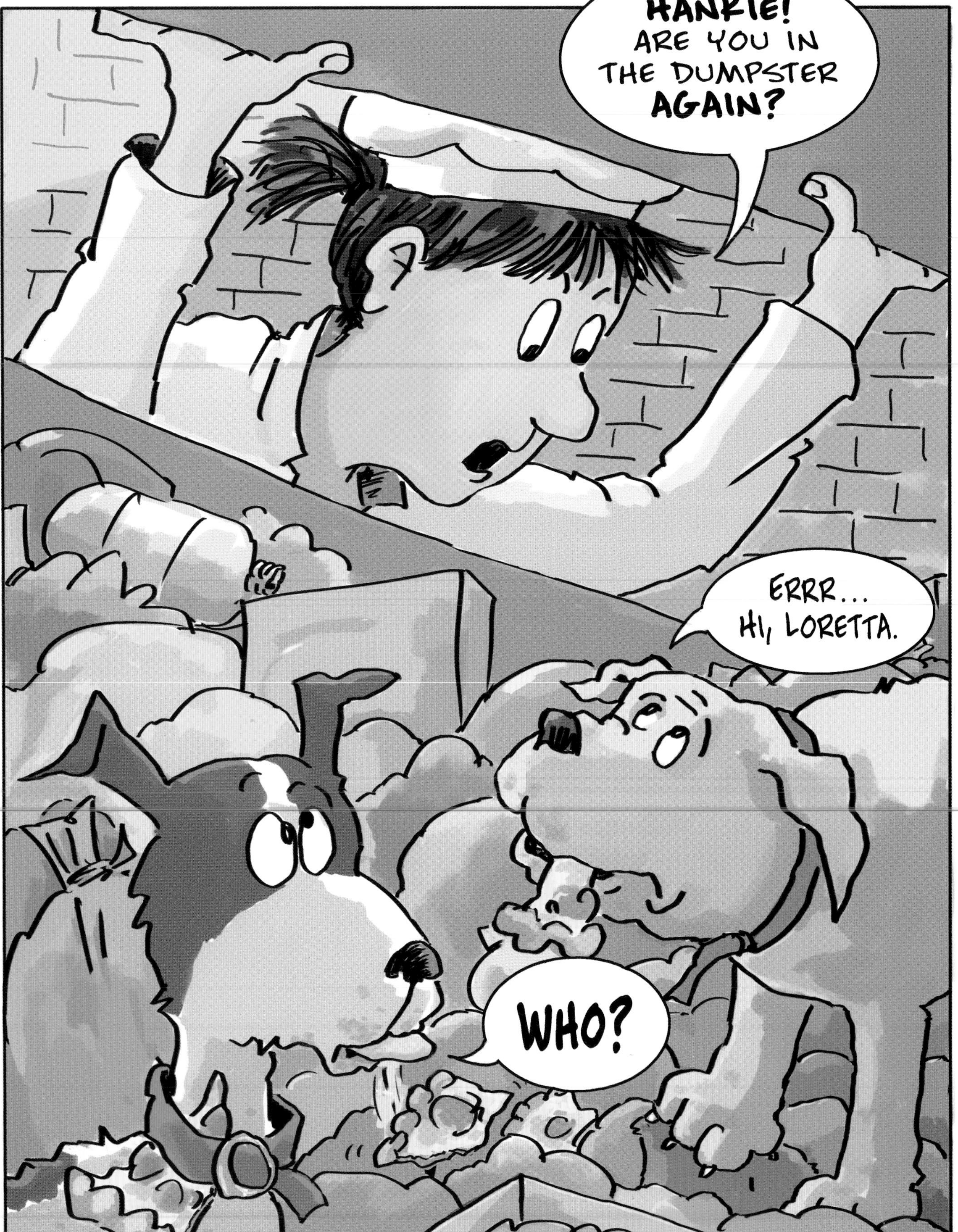
HANKIE! ARE YOU IN THE DUMPSTER AGAIN?
ERRR... HI, LORETTA.
WHO?

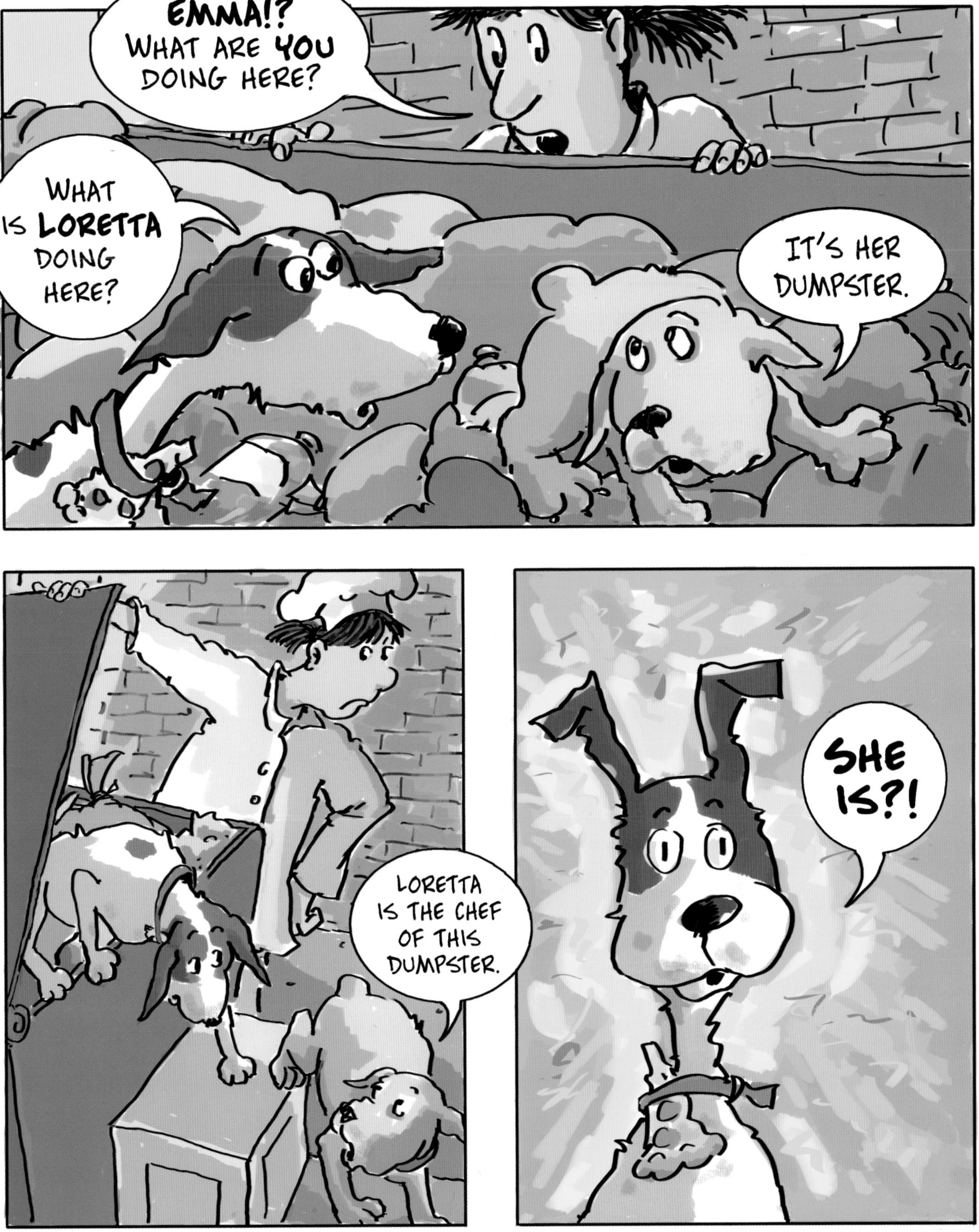
EMMA!? WHAT ARE YOU DOING HERE?
WHAT IS LORETTA DOING HERE?
IT'S HER DUMPSTER.
LORETTA IS THE CHEF OF THIS DUMPSTER.
SHE IS?!

SUDDENLY, I REALIZE LORETTA MIGHT NOT RUIN MY LIFE AFTER ALL.

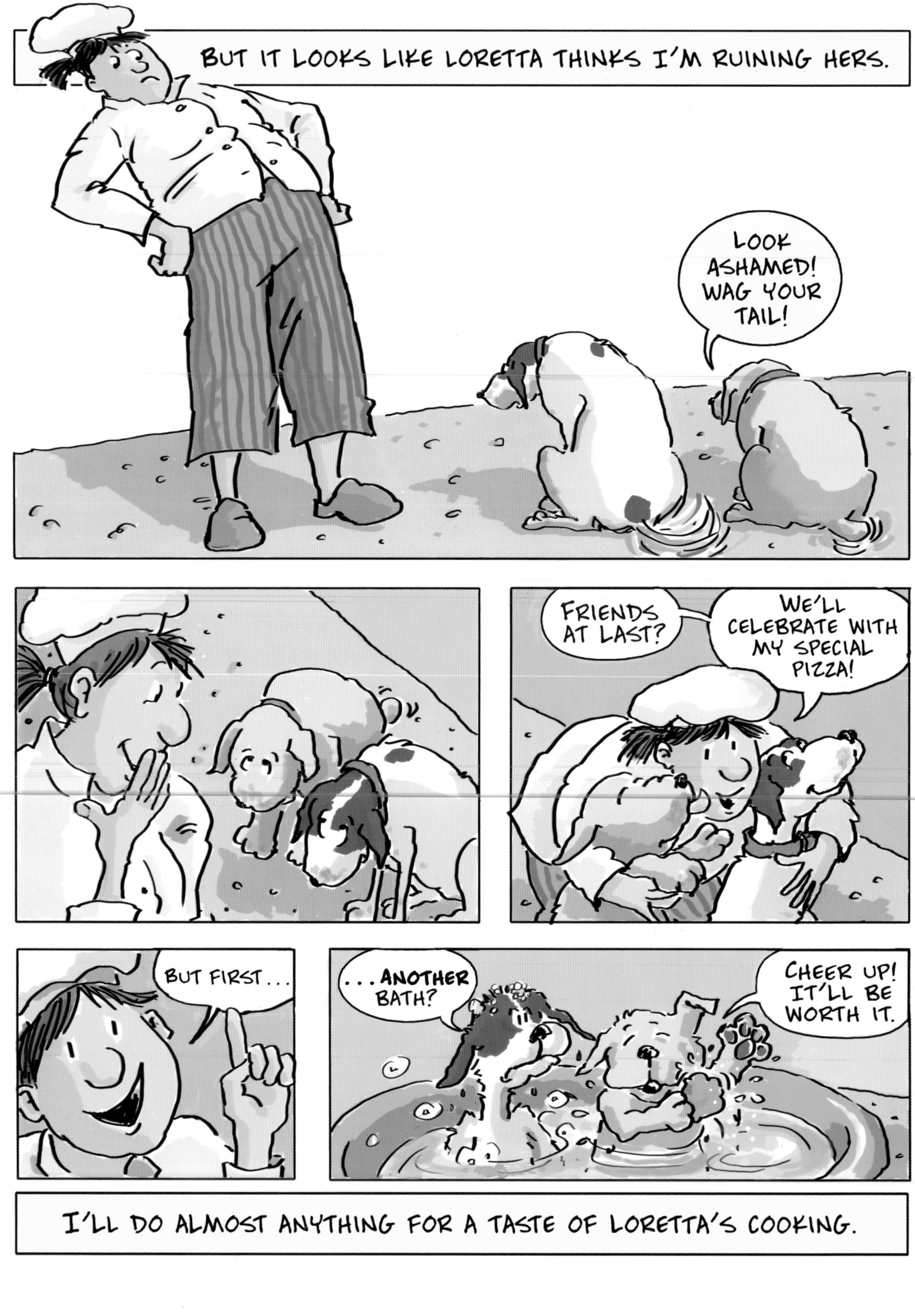
BUT IT LOOKS LIKE LORETTA THINKS I'M RUINING HERS.
LOOK ASHAMED! WAG YOUR TAIL!
FRIENDS AT LAST?
WE'LL CELEBRATE WITH MY SPECIAL PIZZA!
BUT FIRST...
...ANOTHER BATH?
CHEER UP! IT'LL BE WORTH IT.
I'LL DO ALMOST ANYTHING FOR A TASTE OF LORETTA'S COOKING.

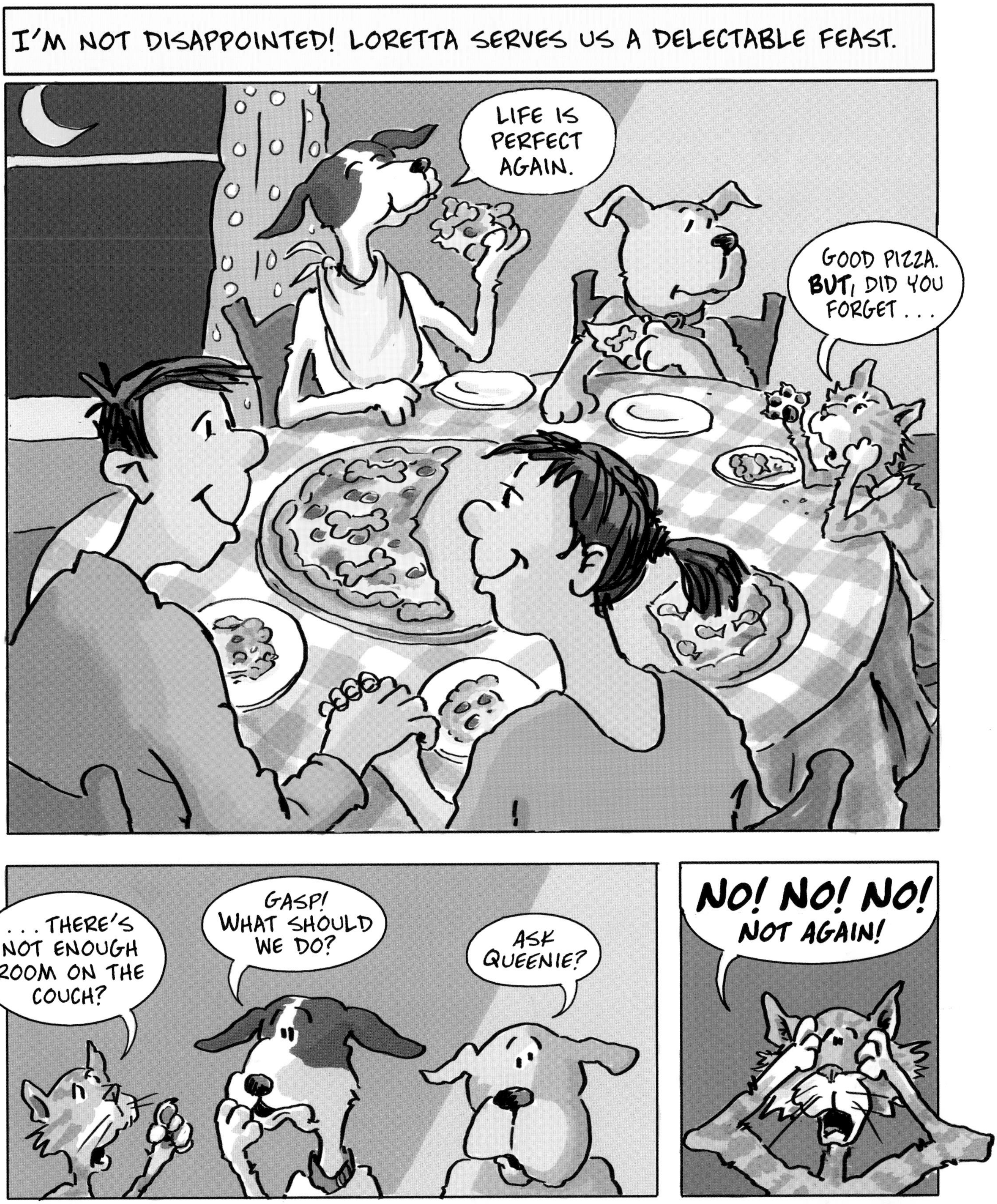
I'M NOT DISAPPOINTED! LORETTA SERVES US A DELECTABLE FEAST.
LIFE IS PERFECT AGAIN.
GOOD PIZZA. BUT, DID YOU FORGET . . .
. . . THERE'S NOT ENOUGH ROOM ON THE COUCH?
GASP! WHAT SHOULD WE DO?
ASK QUEENIE?
NO! NO! NO! NOT AGAIN!
THE CAT IS RIGHT. WE CAN SOLVE THIS PROBLEM OURSELVES.

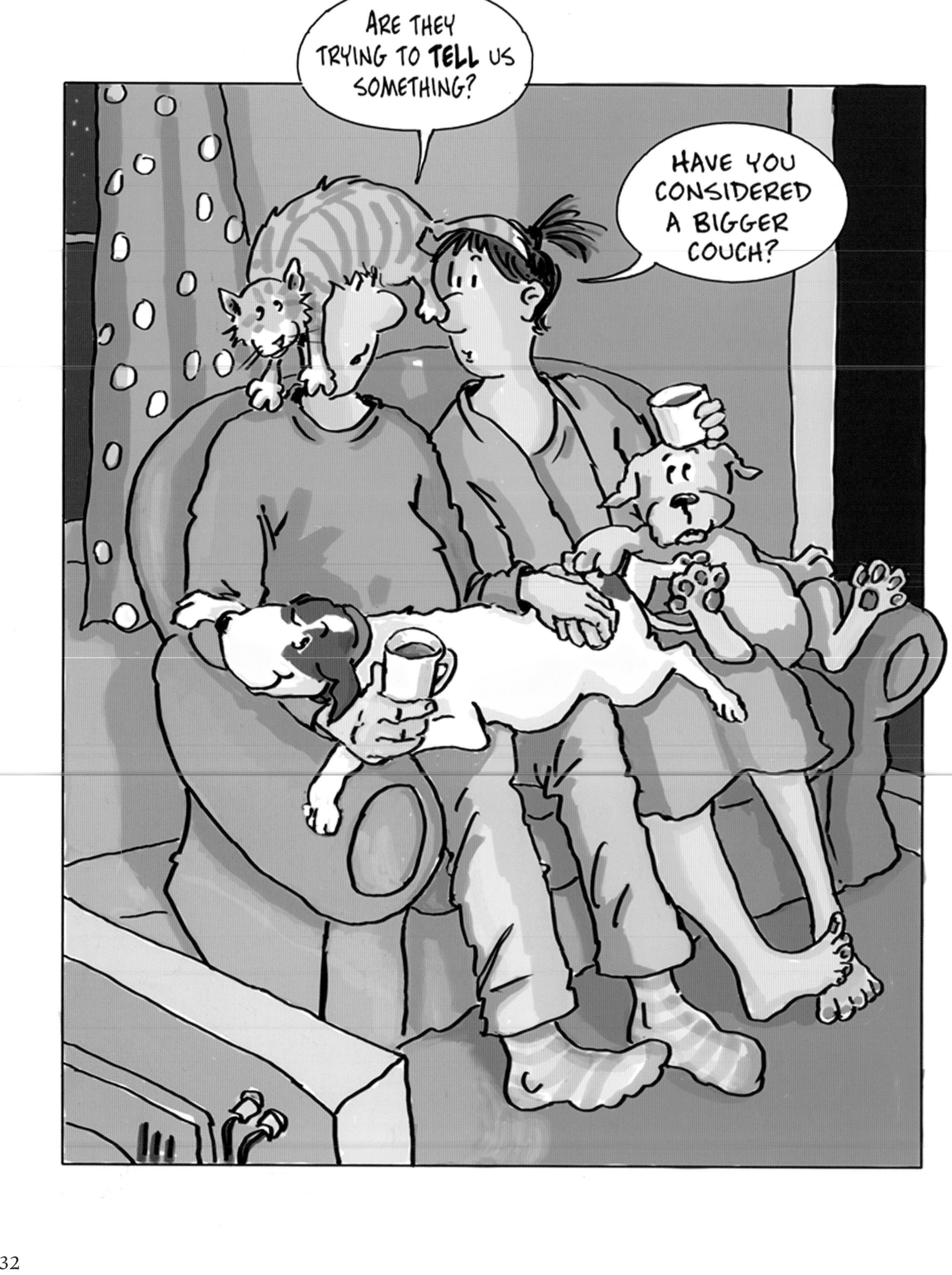
ARE THEY TRYING TO TELL US SOMETHING?
HAVE YOU CONSIDERED A BIGGER COUCH?

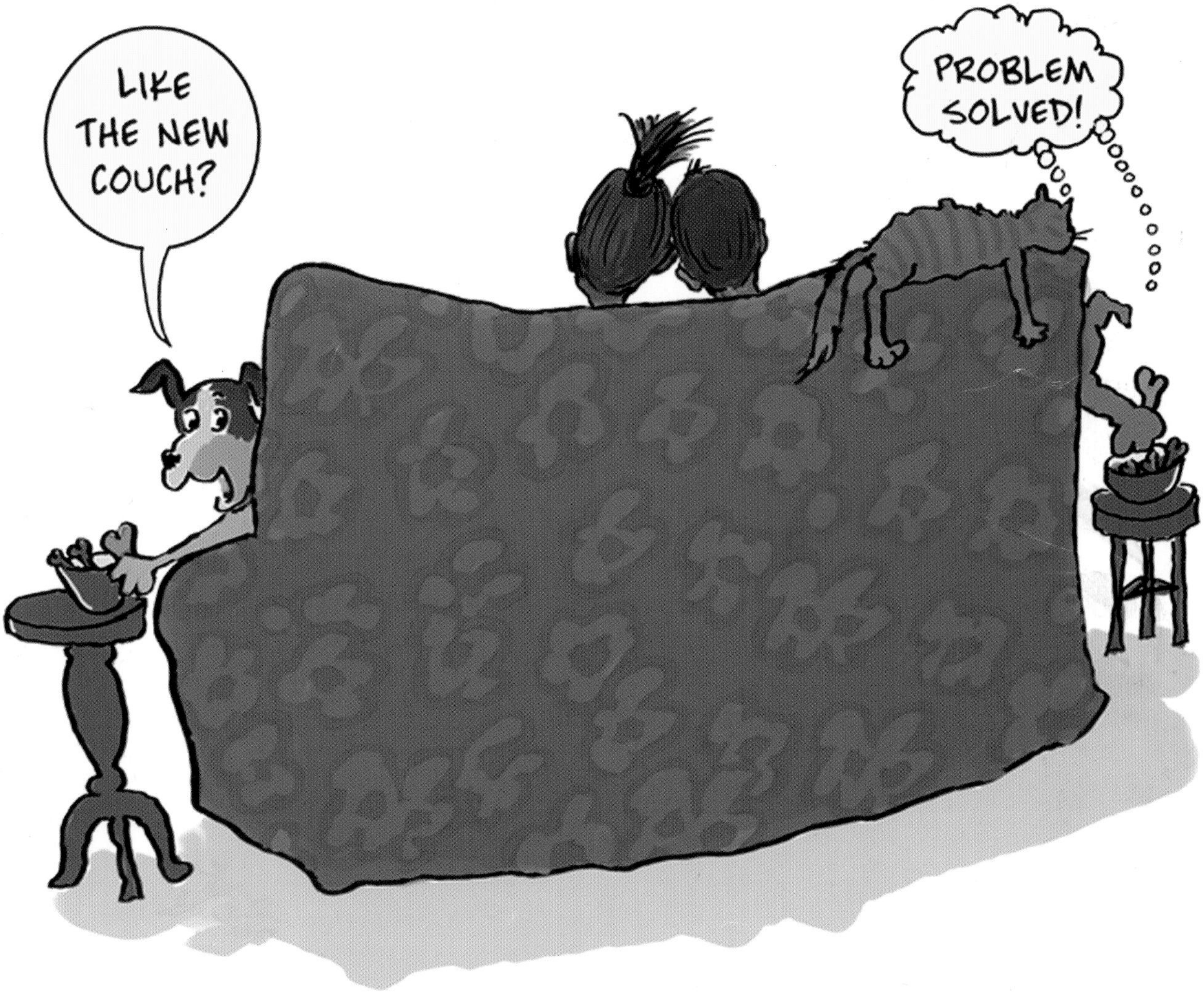
LIKE THE NEW COUCH?
PROBLEM SOLVED!

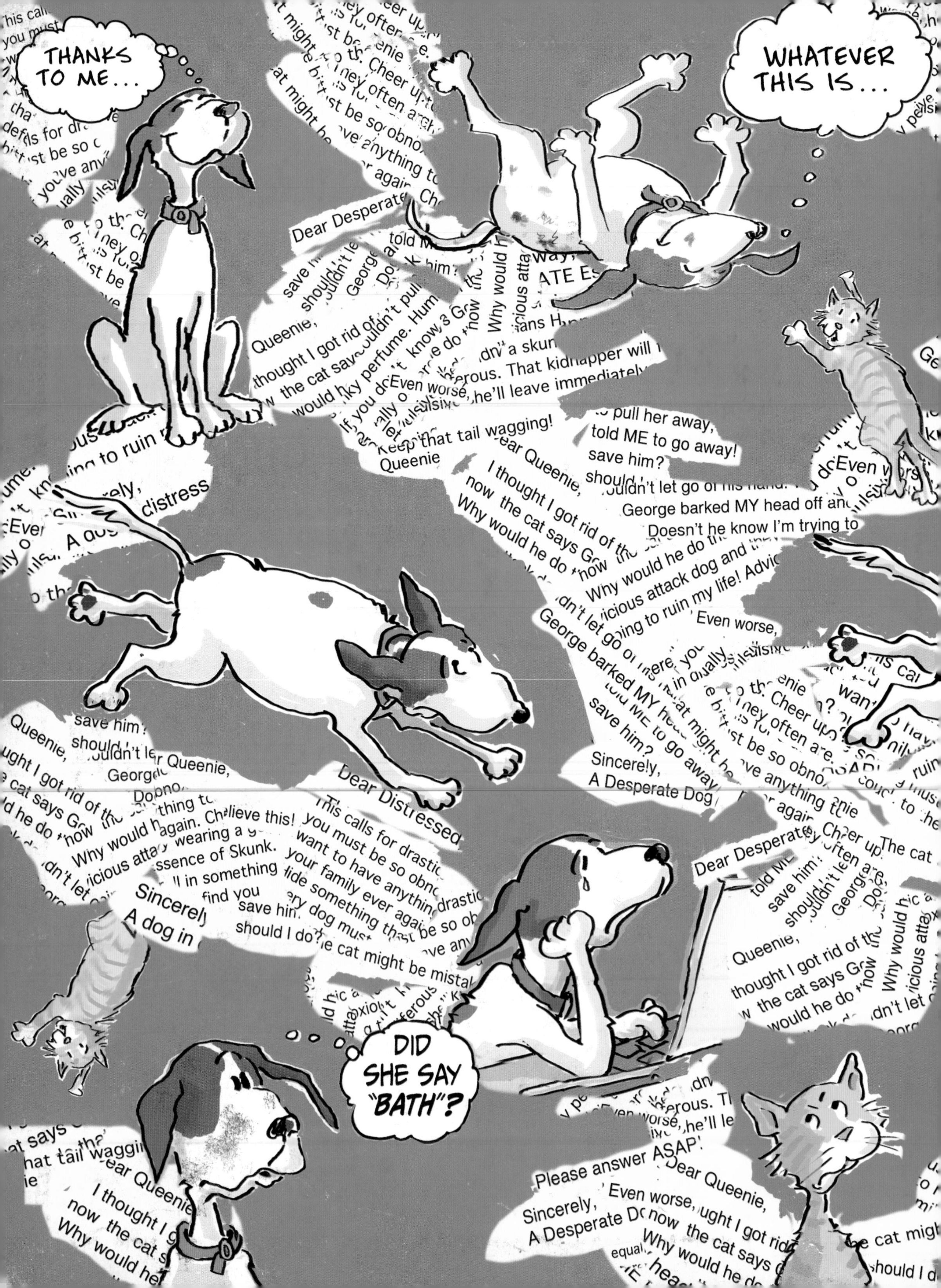
THANKS TO ME...
WHATEVER THIS IS...
DID SHE SAY "BATH"?